WHISKEY PRIEST

Alexander J. Motyl

D1522624

iUniverse, Inc.
New York Lincoln Shanghai

WHISKEY PRIEST

Copyright © 2005 by Alexander J. Motyl

iUniverse books may be ordered through booksellers or by contacting:

iUniverse
2021 Pine Lake Road, Suite 100
Lincoln, NE 68512
www.iuniverse.com
1-800-Authors (1-800-288-4677)

ISBN: 0-595-34367-8

Printed in the United States of America

WHISKEY PRIEST

CHAPTER 1

▼

His first reaction to the sound was indifference. It was only after the cable car lurched backward and began its rapid descent into the valley below that he realized that the cable had snapped. His head crushed against the ceiling, Kanapa turned his gaze at the other passengers. The perfectly coiffed woman in the designer Dirndl was screaming hysterically. Her suntanned husband, wearing a finely woven olive-green loden coat, tightly held her arm with his left hand and his Styrian hat with his right. The Viennese upper class, Kanapa sniffed, always so desperate to look like the *Volk*. But at least they didn't smell like this sodden prole pressed against my leg. Turning away in disgust, Kanapa resolved to focus his mind on more pleasant things. The mountaintops were no longer visible. My deconstruction of sex and furniture, for instance. It will be a smash, I know it. The pine trees had just slipped out of sight and he could make out the leafy crowns of Alpine deciduous trees. But what to call the book? *Is There a Chair in the (Cl)ass?* Too derivative. *Sofa, so Good?* Too jejune. As large boulders came into view, someone let loose a loud fart, and Kanapa, almost gratefully, registered the beginning of the crash that followed.

A cold rain began falling as the Austrian officials conferred. Another accident, they noted, the fifth in the last two years. The country's cables, many of which had been constructed in the interwar period, were evidently in need of repair. Vienna would have to be informed of the province's pressing need for additional funds. They shook their heads as they talked. A crowd of hikers and mountain climbers gathered, stretching their necks to see the corpses. A few arms and legs were visible, traces of clothes and hair lay strewn about, and blood covered much of the wreckage. Policemen walked along the perimeter of the roped-off area, occasionally enjoining some teen-ager to step back. The on-lookers lingered for a few minutes and then, as the rain thickened, began to disperse. Filatov pushed his hands into his coat pockets and moved away with the crowd.

One good deed for the whiskey priest.

As the Riesenrad, the giant wheel that adorns Vienna's Prater park, slowly turned, Clausen took a bite of a hot dog and sat back to enjoy the emerging view. A peculiarly European interpretation of the American staple, he thought, one involving the actual insertion of the frankfurter into a hole in an elongated roll. Was the move reflective of a collective urge to settle sexual scores? Material for a new book, perhaps. Sex as food and food as sex. The topic was hardly original, but there was always something clever to be said about it. He was glad that no one else occupied the cabin. The Viennese annoyed him—their ostensibly polite mannerisms, their lack of backbone, their prejudices, their fatty foods, their over-rated wine. The treetops came into view. These spineless people supported the Kaiser, they supported the republic, they supported their own brand of fascism, they supported Hitler, they supported Waldheim, and now they claimed to support democracy. They supported whoever happened to be in power. He could see the roller coaster and beyond it the rooftops of the second district. The Jews used to live there, and now the district is *judenfrei*. But there is no anti-Semitism in Vienna, absolutely, positively no anti-Semitism. Clausen placed the last bit of sausage into his mouth and wondered how that act could be interpreted—as a homoerotic turn or as a desire for the pleasures of a *ménage à trois*? Of course, it was also just food, but food was as little just food as a cigar was ever just a cigar. The wheel turned a few notches higher and now the Danube was visible. A rapping sound distracted Clausen. As he turned in its direction, he saw a man desperately clawing at the door—how did he get there?—and motioning frantically with his hand. Clausen rushed to his feet and unlatched the door. How curious, he remembered thinking in mid-air, that the man should have tugged so sharply on his arm.

Clausen's mangled body, which had struck the steel beams supporting the Riesenrad, lay at the foot of the giant wheel. The contraption had stopped moving, and a policeman stood over the body.

"*Es war furchtbar!*" said a stout woman. "It was terrible!" She crossed herself. "The door, it swung open and out he fell. I saw him hit the ground. With my own eyes." She pointed at the crumpled heap in the cashmere coat. "*Diesen Mann.*"

The emergency unit clambered out of the ambulance and gathered Clausen's remains. They placed him on a stretcher and carried him to the waiting van. The doors closed, and the policeman told the crowd to go away.

"It's over," he said, "the fun is over. *Der Spass ist vorbei.* Go back to your beer."

An excellent idea, thought Filatov. He walked through crowds of pleasure seekers—past the pickle stands, the go-carts, the pony rides, the House of Horror—toward the Schweizer Haus, one of the Prater's best beer gardens. He found a place at a crowded table, opposite a large woman with an upturned nose and a sullen husband. Filatov raised the mug and, looking at the sun refracted through the liquid, smiled. The dark Budvar reminded him of blood.

Two more good deeds and the whiskey priest could rest.

Sosenko knew where he could best satisfy his sudden craving for baklava—the Naschmarkt, an open-air bazaar a few minutes from his hotel, the Sacher. He took the underground passage that linked the Opera with Karlsplatz, ignored the panhandlers, drunks, and drug addicts, and emerged into the sunlight. The Naschmarkt was crowded with locals—baskets in one hand, children in the other—and tourists gawking at the exotic fruit and inhaling the Oriental smells. Sosenko knew exactly where to go, a small shop, Ali's, about half way down the bazaar and squeezed between a Greek vendor selling barrels of olives and a butcher specializing in horsemeat. He maneuvered past the slow-moving crowds, ignored the Gypsy women with their brown babies and outstretched hands, and stepped into the store with visible relief. The psychology of the mob had fascinated him ever since he had published an annotated edition of Gustav Le Bon's classic. But the mob itself—that was another matter.

"A large piece," he said, pointing to the golden brown pastry behind the counter window. "*Bitte.*"

"*So gross?*" asked the dark-haired man.

"*Genau*, that's exactly the right size."

A minute later Sosenko emerged from the shop. As he placed the pastry into his mouth, ready to savor the sweet taste, he felt a sharp pain in his lower back. Did he pinch a nerve again? His eyes, initially focused on the turn-of-the-century white and green metro station at Kettenbrückengasse, shifted to the multiplicity of colors in the scarf worn by the Turkish woman in front of him. Her black jacket and skirt came into view, followed by her thick calves and dusty shoes. Sosenko slumped to the asphalt, a piece of baklava in his mouth, the rest in his hand.

When the policeman pushed his way through the crowd, the blood from Sos-enko's wound had begun to ooze across the pavement. He turned him over and felt his pulse.

"*Tod*," he announced solemnly to the crowd. "Did anyone see who did this?"

"He bought the baklava in my shop," said the shopkeeper.

"Did anyone see him get stabbed?" the policeman said impatiently. "Did any-one see the killer?"

Leaning against a sausage stand some twenty feet away, Filatov finished his wine and placed the empty glass on the counter. He crossed the Linke Wienzeile and stopped to light a Marlboro in front of the gaudily embroidered art deco buildings. A left at the next street, a right on Gumpendorferstrasse, and he made for the silence of the Cafe Sperl, just up the street. As he stepped inside the chapel-like interior of the solemnly lit V-shaped cafe, he decided against *Guten Morgen* and instead said, "*Grüss Gott*."

One more good deed and the whiskey priest's will would be done.

As it turned out, Igor Alexandrovich Bazarov had been lucky to have drunk too much the night before. He and some of his colleagues, all bored by the con-ference, had gone to Grinzing to imbibe "*etwas Wein*." Some wine turned out to be too much wine, as they went from wine garden to wine garden in search of what Bazarov jokingly referred to as the perfect Traminer. They never found it, but they did get *complétement* drunk, having hooked up with a Belgian journal-ist—a mustachioed man named Adolphe—who bought liter after liter of the young wine while plying them with amusing stories of Jean-Paul Sartre's inconti-nence and Simone de Beauvoir's lesbian affairs. Adolphe also did a hilarious imi-tation of Jürgen Habermas—thick German accent and stutter and all—imitating Monica Vitti's in Antonioni's *L'Avventura*.

As Bazarov reluctantly raised his head from the goose-down pillow, he noticed that it was already past noon. *Merde*, I'll probably miss the tour of St. Stephen's. The conference participants were supposed to be taken into the catacombs and to the top of the spire. The view of the city's first district, of its crazily arranged streets and rooftops, would have been breathtaking. But no matter, it would have to wait until his next visit. Bazarov pushed back the comforter, dropped his leaden legs to the floor, ordered breakfast, and, after opening the thick curtains and wincing at the painful intrusion of light, took a shower and shaved. He looked at his face in the mirror: he was ugly and he knew it. The bushy eyebrows, the nervous eyes, the fat nose, and the thick jowls could not, in any circum-stances, be construed as handsome. But, he smiled while combing back his thick black hair, *that* has never diminished my amorous abilities. Indeed, his physical features may even have enhanced them, creating the impression that his animal magnetism resided solely in his character.

Bazarov opened the door and watched the waiter lower the tray onto the mahogany table near the fireplace. He drank the espresso and, after dipping the *Kipferl* into the little jar of strawberry marmalade, stuffed it into his mouth. A drop fell on his silk tie, and he skillfully removed it with a smoothly rounded fingernail. He grabbed the conference papers scattered on the sofa and took the elevator to the lobby. Several of his friends stood in a circle and, as he could see from the rapid movements of their arms and mouths, they were visibly agitated.

"*Bonjour, mes amis,*" Bazarov smiled. "As the poet said, '*Ach, wie—*'"

"Did you hear?" one of them, Professor Bird, interjected.

"Hear what?"

"Kanapa, Sosenko, Clausen. Dead."

"*Quel horreur,*" said Bazarov. "How?"

"Kanapa's cable car crashed. Clausen"—Bird snickered—"actually fell out of, of all things, the Riesenrad. How's that for drama?"

"And Sosenko?"

"Oh, Sosenko," Bird said absentmindedly. "Sosenko appears to have been stabbed. With a stiletto, right in the Naschmarkt. He had just bought some baklava."

Bazarov turned pale.

"When did this happen? Yesterday?"

"Yesterday, today, the day before yesterday," Bird said. "What difference does it make?" Bird waved to someone across the room. "Are you coming with us to see the cathedral? The others left a few minutes ago."

Bazarov excused himself and ran up the stairs to his room. He closed the door, shut the lock, and let loose a deep breath. His forehead was covered with sweat and his hands were trembling. He walked uncertainly to the minibar and removed four bottles. After he downed all four—he wasn't even sure what he was drinking—he felt a little better. His nerves steadied, he sat down on the sofa and began to take stock of what had just happened.

It was impossible for all three to have died, simply died, in one day. Three unrelated people may, and do, die all the time. That's in the nature of things. That's how probabilities work. But for three of his closest friends and colleagues to have died, and to have died while on a conference in Vienna, could not have been accidental. That is to say, their deaths could not have been coincidental, and if they were not coincidental, then that meant they had been killed. But if they had been killed, then the killer was still on the loose. And that meant he was next.

Bazarov carefully placed a white shirt, underwear, socks, and shaving kit into his alligator briefcase. His passport was where he always carried it, in the breast pocket of his jacket. The tour would begin in a few minutes, and if the killer was waiting for him at St. Stephen's—an ideal place, it occurred to him, to be pushed from the steeple or to be knifed behind some sarcophagus—that meant he had fifteen, maybe twenty minutes to get away. Bazarov decided to leave his other clothes exactly as they were—hanging in the closets and laid out in the drawers. He even turned on his laptop. The killer just might think that he had stepped out, that he'd soon be back. That could win him another hour or two. Bazarov combed his hair and straightened his tie. He left the room, wiped his brow, walked—with nerve-wracking slowness—downstairs, casually said hello to the receptionist, decided against leaving his key—"I'll be back in about an hour," he said—and stepped out of the hotel, even slapping one of his drinking buddies on the back.

He opened the door to the first of the black cabs parked in front of the hotel and told the driver to take him to the airport. As he sat back, he exhaled slowly. He withdrew a gold case from his pocket and removed a thin cigarette.

"*Haben Sie Feuer?*" he asked the driver.

"*Ja, sicher,*" the man said, handing him his lighter. "Turkish?"

"*Ja.*" Bazarov snapped the case shut. "Unfortunately, my last one."

Bazarov took a long drag. They almost got me, but I was lucky. Fortune smiled on me again. It was a mistake. We had gone too far. I knew we had gone too far, but it seemed so easy when Forlini suggested a mutually satisfactory arrangement. A quid pro quo, with no strings attached and no risks. You deliver, we pay. Who could have said no to such an irresistible proposition? It was *too* easy, that was the problem. But not the only problem. That idiot Kanapa had been greedy, and Sosenko had been reckless. But that was no excuse for my own failings. I should have checked Forlini's background and connections. It was obvious that the Italian had betrayed us. Perhaps he thought his cut was too small? It was that idiot Kanapa's fault. I should never have let him negotiate on our behalf. But it was too late now. The damage had been done, and neither Forlini nor Kanapa nor Sosenko nor Clausen was the issue. I am the issue. My survival is the issue.

The cab filled with smoke, and Bazarov opened the window just as it stopped for a red light near the Burgtheater. A large banner announced the world premiere of some play by Thomas Bernhard, the Austrian who hated the Austrians who loved being hated by him. Across the Ring a boisterous collection of colorfully dressed men and women were demonstrating for *Menschenrechte für Schwulen und Lesbier*—human rights for gays and lesbians—in front of the City Hall. A woman with a bullhorn was shouting something incomprehensible with—Bazarov snickered—a man's voice.

The point was—Bazarov took another drag—that you had to know what you're doing, and that idiot Kanapa hadn't. And how could I have been so irresponsibly stupid? It's basic tradecraft. I let Kanapa negotiate with the Italians, while I remained the contact man for the Russians. Kanapa said one thing to Forlini and I said another to Gerasimenko. When Forlini realized that we were sending and receiving mixed messages, he exploited the situation. I would have done the same. As a matter of fact, I *have* done the same. Back in Brezhnev's times, when you could make a pile of rubles by informing *for* the KGB as well as by informing *on* the KGB. All of them thought they were one step ahead—the dissidents figured the secret police would never catch them and the chekists figured they were running the whole show—and he got rich in the process. Or just after he emigrated, when he agreed to spy for the Americans while still in the KGB's employ. But—Bazarov had to laugh—the best part of the story was that he provided both sides with bogus information. The Soviets never denied him an entry visa, while the Americans never minded that he traveled to the USSR so often. Both sides believed he was indispensable, and the irony of it all was that he was, although not quite in the way they thought. I let them play the game they wanted to play, and everyone was happy. Anyway, that worked for as long as it did because I kept both sets of reins in my own hands. What could have moved me to let Kanapa handle the Italians?

The taxi passed the Urania Theatre and the aggressively ugly Ministry of Defense building. The chestnut trees were bare. Vienna's, he recalled, were as often pink as white or yellow. Bazarov looked down the crooked side streets. There were no vanishing points in Vienna, he realized, quite unlike New York. The lines receded with crazy alacrity, but they never disappeared. Somewhere in the maze to his right was Wittgenstein's house. An austere white geometrical structure, not unlike his philosophical system. The Hundertwasser house was also nearby—a multicolored, asymmetrical hodge-podge that resembled his overwrought paintings. Both were unlivable, because both were excessive. Wittgenstein's rejected all feeling, while Hundertwasser's succumbed to all feeling. Was it because both men were Jews? The point was to find a balance—not too much and not too little. That's what that idiot Kanapa violated: he went too far and in going too far he upset the whole enterprise. Bazarov glanced at his Rolex. They would soon be at the airport. Was Kanapa Jewish?

Filatov watched some twenty men and women with briefcases, name tags, corduroy pants, thick long skirts, and knee-length trench coats approach St. Stephen's Square. They were talking loudly. Most of the men had their hands in their pockets. Most of the women wore no make-up. As they paused before the cathedral, Filatov scanned their faces. The man known as Bazarov was not among them. He may simply have decided not to go on the tour, or he may have become suspicious. Either way, there was nothing to do but go to the Sacher.

Filatov turned into Kärntnerstrasse. The shoppers, strollers, and street musicians slowed him down, so he maneuvered along several side streets and, after passing the Cafe Mozart, turned left. He nodded at the doorman and stepped into the lobby. After asking the receptionist if he could use the house phone, he dialed Bazarov's room number. There was no answer. He plunged into the throngs of academics talking about the terrible thing that had happened to poor so-and-so and climbed the stairs to the third floor. He was getting ready to pick the lock on Bazarov's door, when he noticed that it was open. A bad sign. Bazarov must have been in quite a hurry to forget to lock his door. Filatov walked about the room. Everything seemed in place. Silk suits, tasseled shoes, monogrammed shirts, gold cufflinks, Italian ties, striped boxer shorts. The bed was unmade, Bazarov's pajamas lay on the comforter, his slippers stood near the nightstand, the sofa and coffee table were covered with papers, and the computer was on. Filatov stepped into the marble-tiled bathroom. The shower curtain was wet. Soap, towels, shampoo, toothbrush, toothpaste—everything seemed to be there. Except for the razor. That settled it. Bazarov had fled. He'd go to the airport, of course, thinking that he'd be safer taking the first plane out. What he didn't realize was that he'd leave a trail for me to follow. Filatov carefully shut the door, descended the stairs, and walked to the head of the taxi line. "*Nach Schwechat*," he said. The driver turned into the Ring, drove past the monuments and museums, and made a right into the tree-lined street that ran parallel to the Danube canal.

The gray sky pressed down on the orderly arrangement of equally gray buildings on both sides of the canal. The occasional yellow-ochre facade, and the brown roofs straining under the weight of the clouds, only enhanced the feeling of gloom. The canal served no function anymore, except perhaps to add some color—a brackish green—to the monotonous cityscape. He had been to many cities—in Russia, in eastern Europe, in western Europe, even in America—but

Vienna was his favorite. Vienna was self-consciously anguished. Other cities tried to be amusing or charming or carefree, but Vienna seemed to know that death was unavoidable, that misery was at the core of the human condition, and that hope was useless. The Berliners claimed that things might be serious, but not hopeless. The Viennese knew that the truth was just the opposite: things might be hopeless, but not serious. That was it. That was exactly it. We are all doomed, but why worry excessively about it? Why not just have a glass or two of wine and dance the waltz till you fall?

Once on the highway that led to the airport, the taxi slowed to a crawl. The Ost-West Tangente was full of traffic regardless of the time of day. Filatov glanced at his watch.

"*Um wieviel Uhr ist der Flug?*" asked the driver.

"*Macht nichts,*" Filatov said. "There's plenty of time. I can always catch a later flight."

"*Und wohin fliegen Sie?*"

"To Berlin. I'm in construction. I build"—he could not resist saying it—"walls."

Filatov remembered the days when the only way you could get to the airport was by taking the local roads that wound their way past enormous warehouses and compact villages. The airport itself had consisted of one sleepy terminal patrolled by machine-gun bearing soldiers on the lookout for Palestinian terrorists. Those were the days when Vienna was a border town on the front lines of the cold war. Both sides sent their spies to spy on each other. There were no secrets in Vienna—no strategic secrets, that is. Vienna's only valuable secret—that the secret of life was death—was of no interest to Soviet and American war planners and politicians. Perhaps that's why the spies went there? Because it embodied what they knew—that the information they procured was ultimately irrelevant, that nothing really mattered, that not even death mattered?

Filatov shut his eyes. How many times had he killed in Austria? These three made eight. Ironically, the first to die had also been a professor—Aleksandr Alekseevich Zubrov. A leading ideologist for the Russian fascist People's Labor Union, the corpulent *intelligent* had lived in the American zone in Vienna. He composed anti-Soviet books, brochures, and leaflets, and his co-conspirators smuggled them into the fraternal socialist countries as miniature books, microdots, and microfiches. Zubrov liked to frequent the Casanova Club—in those days little more than a cathouse that catered to non-Viennese with access to dollars and foreign passports—in the first district. Filatov laughed as he recalled that

Zubrov had been caught, quite literally, with his pants down. He had shot him in the head—he had been nervous, but one bullet had done the trick—while Zubrov had been screwing some Romanian brunette in a back room. There was no way that his name could not appear in the next day's papers—especially after the top reporter for one of the less scrupulous tabloids received an anonymous tip about the crime. And what a story that had been! Zubrov's fat ass was clearly visible in the photograph, and the headline had identified him as a top Russian nationalist. The fascists had squirmed for months, trying to keep a low profile, explaining to the Austrian police that not all their leaders were sexual perverts. It had been great fun and a great cause.

Now, the killing had ceased being an entertainment—he had certainly tried to be imaginative in his choice of settings—and there no longer was a cause. He recalled the cable car's falling to the ground, the screams, the crash, the shouts. He recalled the slow-motion turning of the Riesenrad, followed by Clausen's rapid flight to the asphalt below. He recalled that he had decided to stab Sosenko at precisely the moment when he had bitten into—and presumably most enjoyed—the baklava. It was like theatre, and he had been the director. The actors had played their parts with great skill, the costumes and scenery had been perfect, and both book and score had been expertly handled as well. And the audience had even applauded. And yet he remained unhappy with his directorial performance. Is this how actors and directors feel when they have nothing left to say? Do you just go through the motions of your art, following the steps without really caring where they lead and why?

It had never been just about entertainment. It had been about belief. And that belief was gone, vanished. A whiskey priest—that is what I am. I fill the chalice with whiskey, because I know that the wine will never become God's blood. And I drink from it, still, eagerly and thirstily, because the ritual is all there is, because nothing else exists. Well, for the time being, Professor Bazarov exists, and hunting him down is some small consolation. The ritual can be reenacted, the play can be staged, the Mass can be held.

The taxi was stuck in traffic again. Filatov opened his eyes and looked out the window. To the right of the highway was the Schwechat oil refinery, a convoluted agglomeration of gleaming silver pipes, tubes, and coils that resembled a human settlement in outer space. Surrounding the refinery were flat fields that only heightened its bizarre appearance. When he first saw it at night, the refinery, bathed in a surreal white glow, had terrified him. He understood now why: the mass of pipes reminded him of Berlin. He had been there, on that awful November day, when the Wall—*die Mauer*—came crashing down.

Everyone was rushing toward the Brandenburg Gate. It could have been May Day, except that they carried hammers and chisels and Trabis, not tanks, clogged the streets. The Alex was also teeming with crowds, some surging toward the radio tower, others toward the Palast der Republik. The Vopos said nothing, did nothing. He stood on Under den Linden, across from the Soviet Embassy. Its gates were shut; soldiers hid in the shadows of the massive building, its silence accentuating the noise of the crowd.

They were dancing on the Brandenburg Gate. They were sitting atop the Wall, hitting it with their hammers, poking it with their chisels, making holes, scars, and indentations, breaking off parts. He walked through the Gate. The Vopos smiled as they waved people through. Someone handed him a bottle of wine. A woman tried to kiss him. He escaped the bearers of gifts and well-wishers. Exhausted, he sat on the steps of the Soviet war memorial and drank the wine. The masses rushed by. Scarves swirled about. The air smelled of beer, wine, and sweat.

What remained of *die Mauer* resembled laundry strung out to dry. The Wall had been reduced to multicolored rags. Enormous holes, jagged and misshapen, broke its surface. No-man's land resonated with an incessant chink-chink-chink. Selling bits and pieces of the Wall had become big business, especially at the Gate and Checkpoint Charlie, where the American hut that guarded their free world once stood. In other parts of Berlin tractors and cranes were busy dismantling the Wall, removing it section by section, first the tube-like structure that adorned the top, then the individual pieces. They lay haphazardly on the ground like toppled gravestones, surprisingly thin for so formidable a barrier, strewn among the empty guard towers that resembled clumps of barren trees in a vast steppe. It was only farther from the city center that the Wall still stood, quietly, secretively, almost embarrassed to be intact.

One year later the Wall was gone. No-man's land had become a vast expanse of empty steppe land. The guard towers had disappeared, and the Trabis, like terrified cockroaches, had fled to the side streets of East Berlin. The Soviet soldiers were gone. The Mercedes had multiplied, scaffolding had appeared, and cranes punctured the horizon. East Berlin was like an emaciated patient, stretched out on a filthy hospital bed, a dirty bedpan near the slippers, the walls cracked, the paint peeling, a thermometer and dog-eared paperback on the nightstand. It was dying, and the doctors and nurses were in the adjoining room, whispering, gesticulating, drinking coffee, and waiting.

The Brandenburg Gate, scrubbed clean, stood bathed in light. He remembered turning left, heading for the vast construction site that used to be no-man's land. The cranes were silent, the traffic flowed in all directions, headlights cast elongated shadows onto the wooden fence. Pipes crisscrossed the sky. He tried following the path of the Wall. It ran along the road. Did it not veer off, slightly, just here? To the left? Or to the right? Eventually it came around to the Gropius Bau, there, but how did it get there? He could look up its exact path in an old map, but the fact of having forgotten disturbed him. It was almost like betraying myself.

Filatov turned away from the refinery and looked at his watch. The taxi was moving. They'd be at the airport in a few minutes.

Tugging at his tie, Bazarov surveyed the departures board. *There*, that's where I'll go. He ran to the Austrian Airlines counter, paid for a first-class ticket in cash, and hurried toward customs. The official opened his passport and slowly examined first the photograph and then his face.

"*Alles?*" He pointed to Bazarov's briefcase.

"*Ja, alles.*"

The Austrian stamped the passport and wished Bazarov "*eine gute Reise.*" Bazarov grunted and rushed into the passengers-only zone. He suddenly felt safe— or, to be precise, safer. Whoever the killer was, wherever he was, he was surely on the other side of the customs barrier. He could, finally, relax. Bazarov ordered a flute of champagne at the Sekt Bar. He downed it as if it were vodka and ordered another. The bartender smiled, "*Schmeckt's?*" Bazarov said nothing, gulping it down with only slightly less alacrity than the first. His hands shook.

"Yes," he said, "it tastes very good. Another one, *bitte.*"

The plane lifted gently into the sky. Bazarov looked out the window at the receding dull fields of Lower Austria. The occasional patch of shimmering water seemed almost shockingly intrusive. The machine circled Vienna and then, after piercing the cloud cover, headed away from the sun. Sitting next to him was an American reading a Bible. A missionary, probably a Baptist. To his front sat two muscular men wearing black shirts and gold necklaces. The stewardesses, all dressed in red skirts, red stockings, white blouses, and red jackets, brought lunch, small trays of coffee, a ham and Brie croissant, and grapes.

"*Kaffee?*" asked a stewardess. He winked at her. A barely perceptible smile appeared on her face. Bazarov took a sip of the coffee and watched her walk down the aisle. Slavic men are never sated, he thought. Sometimes we wonder why God made us that way, but then we just go back to eating and screwing and drinking. The Americans, the Europeans—they always have to justify to themselves that they are alive. As if they needed permission. As if eating and screwing and drinking were unnatural. The stewardess poured him another cup of coffee. As he reached for the cup, he brushed a finger against her nipple.

Bazarov removed a book from his briefcase and opened it. He had begun reading Hans Küng's *Existiert Gott?* several years ago, but had lacked the patience to finish it. The German theologian's critique of Marxism and psychoanalysis wasn't bad, but his own answer to the question was nothing more than a warmed-over version of Blaise Pascal's. If belief in God's existence is a wager and you have nothing to lose from believing and possibly everything to gain, then why not believe? It was a flimsy argument then and an equally flimsy argument now. Besides, it was irrelevant. The real question was "does man exist?" Those awkward agglomerations of molecules were real enough, but weren't they just that? Wasn't man just an invention? A fiction imagined by hyperactive Western thinkers who knew nothing of real life? Bazarov placed the book into his briefcase. There was no helping it. He would never finish Küng's turgid prose or survive his tortured logic. He picked up the other book in the case—*Will the Non-Russians Rebel?* He had bought it at the Vienna flea market, from some scruffy Albanian who, as far as he could tell, specialized in doorknobs, old post cards, bad books, and other junk. The title had intrigued him, even though it posed a rhetorical question that begged an obvious answer—no, never, not in a million years. He slid the book into the pocket beneath the tray. Perhaps a cleaning lady could use it as a doorstop.

The Airbus began its descent through the clouds. Bazarov saw vast green fields, clusters of houses, and anemic roads maneuvering their way shyly through the countryside. Some things never change. The flatness of the landscape, the lazily curving river, the seemingly motionless barges, the rowboats with fishermen, the tiny cars bumping along the dirt roads. After circling the airport several times, the plane skidded along the runway and came to a stop some distance from the main terminal. A wheezing blue and yellow bus pulled alongside the aircraft, and the passengers streamed in. The smell of diesel was the first thing he noticed as the bus sputtered toward the terminal. Bazarov exited the vehicle and walked toward passport control. He was third in line, after an elegant brunette in high heels and a short man in a weather-beaten black leather coat. A sluggish official with an enormous hat and gold stripes looked at Bazarov, flipped through the pages of his passport, and mumbled, "A multi-entry visa?"

Bazarov nodded. "I come here frequently. Business."

"What kind of business?"

"I am a scientist."

"And you are American?"

"*Da.*"

"Born in America?"

"*Nyet.*"

"Where, then?"

"In the Soviet Union. In Odessa."

"Ah," said the man. "Then welcome home, Dr. Bazarov."

The departures area at Schwechat was packed with travelers. Americans in sneakers and jeans, Austrians in jackets and ties, Jews in long coats and felt hats, Arabs in flowing robes, Russians with mobile phones attached to their ears. Filatov did not even bother to check the many faces. Bazarov would be long gone. There was also no point in examining the departures board to determine where he might have gone. Instead, Filatov took the stairs to the airport security office located behind a nondescript door on the second floor. He strode up to the clerk manning the phones and shoved a sheaf of papers and a badge at him. The visibly flustered Austrian replaced the receiver and adjusted his glasses.

"*Ja?*" This time, he tugged at his beard.

"I would like to see Hans Meyerhof."

"Herr Doktor Meyerhof is busy. Perhaps you would like to make an appointment?" The tall, broad-shouldered man standing before him was probably an American businessman. He could wait.

"Look at my papers."

The clerk began rustling through the documents and then stopped.

"You are with the—?" he inquired cautiously.

"—the FSB," Filatov replied. "The Federal Security Service of the Russian Federation. The former Committee for State Security. The KGB."

The clerk cleared his throat. "*Ein Moment, bitte.*"

An Austrian socialist formerly on the KGB's payroll and a protege of the redoubtable Bruno Kreisky, Hans Meyerhof could still be relied on to help his old friends from the east—especially those who had helped him buy a summer villa off Neusiedlersee in the Burgenland. He had even been gracious enough to let his Russian friends use the villa for a variety of purposes, both recreational and professional. Filatov had been there once, after kidnapping some Lithuanian fascist and keeping him imprisoned in the wine cellar until he signed a declaration denouncing his movement. He had been killed afterwards, and his body had been buried in Meyerhof's cherry orchard. I wonder if he knows?

Twenty minutes later Filatov emerged from Meyerhof's office. Meyerhof had assured him that the Austrian people were always happy to assist the fledgling Russian democratic state in tracking down smugglers. Contraband was an outrage. A transgression against rule of law, a transgression against democracy, indeed, a transgression against civilization itself. Here were the passenger lists from every flight that had departed Schwechat in the last three hours. Would that be enough? Would Herr Filatov require anything else? Would he like to stay free of charge in the airport hotel? Always ready to be of assistance, *mein lieber Herr.* And how nice it would be if one's services were to be rewarded—nothing extravagant of course, times were different of course, but life was life, was it not, and there were so many mouths to feed and so many needs to be met.

Five minutes later Filatov was on the phone to Kiev. Next morning he stepped into the same blue and yellow bus that had transported Bazarov to the Boryspil terminal.

CHAPTER 2

▼

"Still reading that trash, Jane?" Allen Bristol pointed to a Mickey Spillane paperback on her desk. "Don't you know that humanity moved on past monosyllabic literature several thousand years ago?

"By the way, Jane," he continued, "the boss wants you. Pronto. Seems like culture is heating up again."

"Go to hell," Jane Sweet said as she walked past Bristol's desk. "And who the hell says pronto anymore?"

Allen Bristol, the deputy to the deputy for something or other at the embassy, a snooty Ivy League graduate, a child of privilege, a family friend of the Kennedys, a denizen of St. Moritz and Vale, a connoisseur of fine wines, a subscriber to *The New Yorker*, a man who wore Brooks Brothers clothes and favored bow ties and suspenders. My opposite, she thought, in almost every way. Is that why I think he's an idiot or is he really an idiot?

Jane walked up the broad marble staircase. After saying hello to the secretaries arrayed on both sides of the anteroom, she tapped on the door and walked in. The American ambassador to Austria was a thick-set man of about fifty-five, a cattleman who had contributed millions to the president's campaign and, instead of being rewarded with London, Paris, or Rome, found himself in post-imperial Vienna amidst its genteel mannerisms and incomprehensibly social democratic ways. Jane disliked him from the moment he arrived, three months ago, to replace the career foreign-service officer who had served as ambassador for the last seven years. The feeling, she knew, was mutual.

"We have a situation, Sweet," he said. "You hear about them three guys that died?"

"Yes, sir. Two had freak accidents, and the third seems to have been knifed in the Naschmarkt."

"The Austrian *Po-li-zei*"—he pronounced the word *poe-lee-zigh*—"think it might be a series of murders. Some academics in Vienna have too much to drink and the Austrian fucking *Po-li-zei* think it's murder."

"Is it, sir?"

"We don't know, Sweet." He sat back in his chair. "But I want to find out before Washington gets involved."

"Shouldn't the CIA look into this?"

"They're busy." He leaned forward again. "But you're not. Should be a piece of cake."

"I'm the cultural attaché, sir," she protested. "I'm not a field agent. I don't do this kind of thing. You know I don't."

The ambassador lowered his eyes to an open file and Jane understood that she was to say nothing. He leafed through several pages and focused his gaze on her.

"Did you ever wonder"—he held up one of the pages—"did you ever wonder why State took you in? I mean, what with all those relatives of yours in Russia, you're a pretty big security risk."

"I figured I slipped through the cracks, sir."

"More like *pushed* through the cracks, Sweet."

"I don't understand, sir." But I do, she thought, but I do.

"Think, Sweet."

"Because I'm a woman."

"Bingo, Sweet." His voice trailed away. "So stop acting like one."

Jane closed the door behind her and met the half-concealed smirks of the secretaries. They had been listening of course, and the harridans were glad that she had gotten an upbraiding. She ran her fingers through her hair, pulled it back, and returned their smirk. What bullshit, she thought. I am working with idiots and I am working for idiots. And Vienna isn't even a hardship posting.

As soon as he saw her, Bristol placed the book he was reading face down on his desk and smiled sweetly.

"You look like you've been to the woodshed, Jane. Anything I can do to help?"

"Oh, go to hell," she snapped, taking her jacket, dropping the Spillane in her pocket, and walking out.

Bristol cocked his head to watch Jane leave. She was wearing gray pants with a frilly red blouse and white pumps. Her blond hair, which was usually tied back in a ponytail, fell down to her shoulders and into her eyes. Two years in Vienna, and she still dresses like an American tourist. Her face was nice enough, he supposed, a bit too round, but with high cheekbones and full lips and a large forehead. Add a thick skirt, kerchief, and hayfork, and she could pass for one of those absurdly healthy women in the socialist realist paintings the Communists loved so much. Except that those women were always smiling.

Jane shut the embassy door behind her. She went down Boltzmanngasse, made a few turns, and arrived at the Strudelhofstiege, a delicately structured series of zigzagging staircases built in the days when Vienna was an imperial capital. Soon after her arrival in the city, she had begun reading Hugo von Hoffmannsthal's novel of the same name, but after struggling through some fifty pages had reluctantly decided that her German, however good, just wasn't quite that good. It seemed like such a long time ago. The promise of romance, the threat of intrigue, had quickly turned into routine. Worst of all, her colleagues annoyed her. The ambassador deserved to be shoveling the horse shit on St. Stephen's Square; Bristol, that arrogant little snit, might just have the smarts to tend bar in the Hamptons. All the others were ambitious little bureaucrats, monotonous men and women who carried on about their silverware and promotions and children. The embassy was a microcosm of an American suburb—neat lawns, identical houses, vast malls, faceless restaurants. And overweight people in striped shirts, baggy shorts, and floppy hats. What would Mike Hammer do in my place? He'd shovel down some eggs, have five beers, call everyone a jerk, and shoot them all. Jane paused in the middle of the stairs, closed her eyes, and smiled.

"Oh, hell," she said, and climbed into a cab at the corner. "The Ministry of Education, bitte."

Several hours later Jane knocked again on the ambassador's door. He was sitting on the leather sofa, his right leg balanced precariously on his left knee. A plump hairless calf looked out from between the cuff and woolen checkered sock.

"Well, sir," she began, "seems like all three men were academics—"

"I know that, Sweet."

"—and all three were Russia specialists, and all three were friends—"

The ambassador placed his left leg on his right knee. Good God, his socks didn't match.

"—and all three were involved in the same research project. Something about building civil society in the former Soviet Union." Jane forced herself to look away from the socks. "And all three were here for the same conference. It's at the

Academy of Sciences, sir. Something about democracy and markets in eastern Europe."

"Are we paying for this crap?"

"USAID, sir. Lots, too. They're all staying at the Sacher."

"The Sacher? That's three hundred a night."

"Four hundred, sir." Jane smiled. "Anyway, the conference isn't over, so I'll go there tomorrow and talk to some of the participants."

The ambassador pointed at his desk clock.

"I've got a better idea, Sweet. Why don't you go out with the boys tonight? Show them a good time."

As she placed her hand on the doorknob, he added, "Welcome to the real world, Sweet."

"Got to hell," she shouted back—very, very silently.

The sky was turning a sullen gray. The cab ride to the Sacher would take about ten minutes, but Jane decided to make a brief detour down Gumpendorf-erstrasse and have a *Tee mit Zitrone* at the Sperl. Her act of passive resistance was pathetic, she knew, but it was better than heading straight for the hotel. She would sip the tea slowly, suck the lemon wedge, and, after casually perusing some newspaper, saunter over to the Sacher.

She found a seat at the very back—her favorite table, which afforded her a view of the whole cafe and the street outside. She had watched Vienna change through that window. Once upon a time statues, monuments, and buildings used to be black from smog and automobile exhaust; courtyards had cracked tiles; walls had peeling plaster; the ochres were almost charcoal; the reds resembled sunsets; cobblestone streets consisted of real cobblestones; the seats in the Sperl were worn and sagging. She recalled how, when she first came to Vienna in the seventies, she had left the Sperl, strolled down the preposterously named Gumpendorferstrasse for two or three blocks, and come upon a crumbling stair-case on the right. At the top, a nondescript dark green door opened onto a dank passage that led her up stairs and courtyards, past clotheslines and public sinks, past weed-covered cobblestones, past cracked walls and crumbling paint, past ancient mailboxes with barely visible names scribbled into the tiny openings, and ended in another metal door that opened onto Mariahilferstrasse and a small the-atre showing pornographic films. The passage had long since been cleaned and scrubbed and painted, its nooks were now occupied by galleries and wine bars. That staircase had also been renovated, the rust-covered iron railing had been replaced, the steps were flat. She recalled that, several years ago, they had even tried renovating the Sperl. They had painted the walls, replacing the years of smoke with a luminous ochre. They had installed new chandeliers and new seats, and they had removed a faded mirror that hung in the back. But the Sperl had fought back and, within a few years, the grime and soot and sagging seats had returned. Things are what they are, Jane thought. They can be cleaned and caressed, cherished and remembered. But things have a life of their own. Things are like words and numbers. You can arrange and rearrange them as much as you like, but they order themselves according to their own logic anyway. Is that fatalism? Or is that just fate?

"*Einen Tee mit Zitrone, bitte,*" she said to the waitress. Her eyes skimmed the *Frankfurter Allgemeine Zeitung,* straining at the densely packed print unrelieved by any graphic design. The grayness blinded her, making it impossible to concentrate. The waitress placed the small tray—a glass of tea, a small spoon, a slice of lemon, and three cubes of sugar, two white and one brown—on her table. Jane squeezed the lemon and watched the tea turn a brighter shade of orange-brown.

The glow of the setting sun, the smell of the grill, beer cans on the grass, her mother and father and grandmother sitting in white lawn chairs. Talking, always talking, always talking about the same things they always talked about. The war. The *Bolsheviki.* The Germans. Who died. Who lived. Who fought. Who escaped. Where they escaped to. How they escaped. The trains. The camps. The war, the war, the war. Always the same conversation, with each adult taking turns saying the same things the others had just said. Their conversation was like a constant drone, whether of planes or birds or traffic. It was like being trapped in a car with the three of them, caught in endless rows of cars and trucks inching their way down the Long Island Expressway.

The standard refrain—tato's. From about the middle of June, her father says, life was no longer normal. Trains were slowly moving west. Schools were being refitted with sanitary equipment. Rumors flew about. Would there be war with Germany? When would the Soviet occupation finally end? *How I hate your rhetorical questions, tato.* Sunday morning, I was getting ready to leave the house, when my neighbor told me that war had broken out. How did he know? *Probably heard it on CNN.* Was this just another rumor? *Of course it wasn't, you know it wasn't.* I made for the university. Along the way the public speakers announced that Molotov would be making a statement later that day. I ran home. We turned on the radio and heard him denounce Germany's surprise attack on our "fatherland." All of us—the lodgers, the landlady, and her three sons—looked at one another in disbelief. Then we began talking. What wonderful news, we all said.

Bad call, folks. The Germans couldn't lose. *Oops.* Slavko, the landlady's oldest son, couldn't sit still. Come, he said to me, let's go outside. We went to his relatives. They were as excited as we were. But when we returned home, the mood had changed. Everyone began to worry about the future. *About time, tato.* Then came the news of my neighbor's arrest. I decided to spend the night in the woodshed. At midnight the landlady rushed in: the NKVD had also arrested Slavko. *So much for ol' Slavko, eh?* Next day I went to work. The office was quiet, everyone was visibly nervous, jumping at the slightest squeak of the doors. Then Petrov, our boss, walked in. Comrades, he said to us in Russian, the Hun has attacked our homeland. I do not want to live without communism. At that moment the door opened and in walked my landlady's youngest son. The slip of paper in his hand told me that I had been drafted into the Red Army. They gave us a rifle, a bayonet, a knapsack, boots, and a uniform. Then they loaded us into the trains heading east. *Sayonara, tato.*

Do you remember? someone else says. The planes came at all hours of the day. The bombs fell near the town. One hit the cemetery, destroying several graves and scattering bones and decomposed bodies. We collected them that same day and placed them in makeshift graves. *Oh God, not this part, I hate this part.* When the Germans passed through our village, another voice—mama's? tato's?—says, they caught a few peasants and hanged them. Later, some children found an unexploded grenade near the river, but when they tried to pry it open, it exploded and killed them. *Oh God, stop it!* The war rolled across the village, first eastward, then westward, then eastward again, then westward. After a while, the soldiers all looked alike—their uniforms covered with mud, their helmets filthy and dull, their gate slow and lizard-like, their faces empty, and their eyes blank. We would hide in our homes when the soldiers came. We would hide our livestock in the forest, bury our grain, and slaughter our chickens. The young men would run into the woods, raising their legs high as they rushed through the tall grass past the cemetery. And when the soldiers were gone, the old women would run past the cemetery, through the tall grass, and into the wood, whispering at first, and then crying, It is safe, come out, come out, they are gone. The second time war came, the woods no longer offered refuge. You could still hide, but if you did, there was no coming back. Occupation was almost worse than war, someone says. *I don't care. Do you hear me? I decidedly do not care.* In war, there were spaces between the fronts. During the occupation, there was no place to go. The Wehrmacht controlled the countryside, the Sicherheitsdienst and SS rooted out the opposition, and the collaborators joined the Polizei. *You mean the poe-lee-zigh, don't you?*

What could we do? someone says. We had no choice. Yes, someone else says, we had no choice. I was walking home when suddenly the women cried, Run, run, the police are rounding up workers. I turned into a building, crossed the yard, and hid behind the staircase, in the toilet. I remember standing on the wet concrete floor, holding my handkerchief to my nose, clutching my bag to my pounding chest. I heard footsteps, cries, and shouts in the street. And a gunshot. Was somebody killed? *Of course someone was killed, you know that.*

Nothing is visible inside the rattling train car, a voice says. No cracks of light break the monotony of the darkness. The sobbing, the crying, the whispering form a constant hum, a buzz that never subsides, never goes away. *Like your damned memories.* People soil themselves where they sit. The stench commingles with the sounds to produce an all-enveloping blackness, a sense of hopelessness, of despair. At first they try not to fart when they defecate. *Not the shit story again!* After several days people fart even when they don't shit. Our stomachs rumble, we belch and spit and snort. No one pays any attention, no one minds. Our joints ache, our backs are stiff, our hair sticks to our sweaty foreheads. The train ignores us, moving relentlessly east. *But this is where I get off.* When we finally stop, when the doors slide open, and light and air rush in like waves, we blink and gasp, moving our arms above our heads, turning toward the light, pouring out as if we were sand. The people see the stains on their pants and skirts, the women try to hide the blood running down their legs, the men grab the seat of their trousers. *Not me. I've got clean clothes. See?* Everyone stamps about nervously, looking at the ground, tending to the children, not speaking, not looking into other people's eyes. The *Bolsheviki* bark commands, shoving the men with their rifle butts and screaming obscenities at the women. They force us down the platform, push us into waiting black trucks, and shut them tight. The trucks ride for hours along rough roads, knocking the men and women against one another, making everyone aware of their stench and filth. The trucks finally stop on an empty plain, where only one or two barracks stand. We are told to climb out. This is where you will live, say the guards. But there is nothing here, someone says. So build yourselves villas, the guards laugh. *Leave, leave, please leave that awful place.*

The beer cans are collected, the chairs are folded and placed into the shed. There is supper and television and Walter Cronkite and more talk—about the same things, always about the same things.

"*Zahlen, bitte,*" Jane said and placed two Euros on the table.

She looked up at the Sacher's imposing facade. Jane had visited the Sacher Cafe only once and had been aghast at the prices. Eight-dollar coffees and twelve-dollar cakes. She recalled watching a stuffed-shirt waiter push a cart toward the table next to hers. As the russet-haired gentleman and his young escort giggled, the waiter lifted the cover from the silver tureen, carefully dipped an over-sized fork into it, and removed a pair of frankfurters. That must have cost twenty-five dollars, she had thought. The man then opened a jar of Grey Poupon mustard, smeared a bit onto his plate, and, after taking the wurst into his right hand—his pinky extended—brushed it against the mustard and, in one elegant motion, raised it to his lips. The young man sitting across from him had turned red, taking a long sip of wine and looking in her direction. Then, amazingly, he winked at her and Jane, unsure of how to react, had raised her glass and said, "*Prosit!*" The older man looked at her with disdain, while his partner broke into a deep laugh.

Since those early days Jane had learned more about the Viennese and their bizarre ways. She had learned that their extreme politeness was often a disguise for an even more extreme viciousness. That the aggression they felt toward the world was really directed at themselves. That the bonhomie they displayed was also a refuge from suicide. That they were as opportunistic as they were principled and that they were as principled as they were opportunistic. That they always lied and always told the truth. That they were both direct and indirect, but that you never quite knew which was which and when. The Viennese were a walking contradiction, a living paradox. Everything and its opposite, and all shades in-between, was true about them. They should, Jane figured, just fall over. Nothing built that way could stand, let alone survive. Instead, they managed to walk and talk and even dance. It was an amazing performance, one that she never tired of watching. And it was such a welcome contrast to the sameness of Long Island—which was not only her birthplace, but a state of mind and a condition of existence. *Die echte Wiener*—the real Viennese—would die if forced to live there. Small wonder that many of the Americans who worked in the embassy never dared venture into the real Vienna, preferring the safe confines of their little bit of home and their stately apartments in the nineteenth district. After a few months in that ex-pat no-man's land Jane had moved to the seventh district, an old part of old Vienna, located behind the Parliament and City Hall, a place favored by Balkan immigrants, students, prostitutes, bums—and, increasingly alas, well-heeled yuppies. Where you could still get an enormous pork Schnitzel and a large glass of young wine for a fraction of what they cost elsewhere, where the store signs were faded relics of a past age, where communal toilets still adorned the hallways.

The last of that day's sessions had ended a half-hour ago, and Jane expected the academics to be returning to the hotel before going to dinner. She entered the richly adorned lobby and sat on an easy chair flanked by two potted palms. The staid *Die Presse* had a lead article about the three deaths. The Austrian authorities suspected foul play, but no one could explain why three run-of-the-mill American professors should have been killed. One columnist suggested that they might have been the targets of a terrorist attack, vaguely hinting at Middle Eastern involvement. A tabloid raised the possibility that *die Amerikaner* might have been members of some weird cult. Jörg Haider, the body-sculpting, perpetually tanned right-winger, repeated his campaign slogan: Vienna dare not become Chicago! The *International Herald Tribune* devoted a straightforward page-three story to the killings, under the heading "Three U.S. Professors Killed in Austria." The *Wall Street Journal Europe* ignored the incidents altogether, presumably on the rationale that they were a distraction from the good news coming from the initial public offerings sweeping the telecommunications industry.

Three haggard men with name tags walked into the lobby. Loaded down with papers, books, and briefcases, they crossed to the chairs next to Jane and sat down. One of them, bifocals perched on his long nose, pointed at *Die Presse* and said, "Terrible thing, that. Just terrible."

"Did you know them?" Jane asked. He was thin, had a long sallow face and unusually large ears, and sported a dark green knit tie with his button-down striped shirt.

"Oh, yes. Quite well."

"By the way, I'm Jane Sweet, cultural attaché at the U.S. Embassy here."

"Ah, a spook."

"No, not at all. Maybe during the cold war. Nowadays a cultural attaché is just a cultural attaché."

"No kidding. My name is Bird. Jack Bird. Professor at New York University. I do Sovietology. Or post-Sovietology as we call it now. Of course, who the hell knows what we call whatever we do.

"I'm sorry," he added somewhat absent-mindedly. "That's neither here nor there."

"The ambassador asked me to look into this," Jane said. "What do you think? About the killings, I mean."

"Dunno. I didn't like them, actually. Thought they were all pricks. But that could just be academic politics. Who knows. By the way, who's the ambassador? Some rich guy, right?"

"I heard they were involved in some project. Anything important?"

"Oh, you know, the usual. They got some big money—and I mean really big money—to save the world. Or is it to save Russia? Who knows." Bird looked around the room. "So tell me about the ambassador. Hear he's an asshole. That right?"

"Is that unusual?"

"How am I supposed to know? You work for the guy."

"I mean getting that kind of money."

"Nah, happens all the time. Wished it happened to me. No kidding." Bird turned to his colleagues and laughed.

"This here," he continued, "is Al Ratter, a Harvard prof, and that's Sy Sobaka, of Yale." Ratter, a big man with carefully arranged strands of hair on his otherwise bald head, grinned. Sobaka, dressed in jeans and sneakers, flashed a set of brilliant white teeth.

"Did you gentlemen know the deceased?" Jane asked.

They nodded.

"I knew Kanapa," said Ratter. "Quite well."

"I was close to Sosenko," said Sobaka.

"And we all hated them!" added Bird.

"May I ask why?" Jane said.

"Arrogant sons of bitches," replied Ratter.

"Motherfuckers," mumbled Sobaka.

"Assholes," said Bird.

"Not very popular with the profession, were they?"

"Damn right they weren't," said Bird. "Everybody hated them. Especially Bazarov."

"Bazarov?" Jane asked. "Who's Bazarov?"

"Bazarov's their buddy," said Bird. "I mean *was* their buddy. He led the project. Got the money. They just did what he told them to do."

"Like all good critical thinkers." Ratter winked.

"So where's this Professor Bazarov? I'd like to meet him."

"Who knows," Bird replied. "Haven't seen him since yesterday."

"We're about to have dinner," Sobaka said. "A Lebanese restaurant. Supposed to be pretty good. Want to come?"

Not in a million years, pal.

The Herrengasse was a narrow street that extended from the Opera to Schwedenplatz, near the University. On the way Ratter and Sobaka fell into a heated conversation. Jane heard only isolated words—subjectivity, post-colonialism, the imaginary, difference—but noticed that, whenever they were articulated, voices were invariably raised. Bird rolled his eyes and poked his tongue in his cheek.

"They go on like this all the time," he said wearily. "No kidding."

As they approached Josefsplatz, he took Jane by the forearm and stopped.

"Did you know that this is where they filmed—"

"—*The Third Man*. Yes, I know. It's in all the guide books."

"No kidding?"

The space before the arched entrance to the Imperial Palace, the Hofburg, was teeming with tourists. Horse-drawn *Fiakers* inched their way along the streets, their drivers dressed in top hats, colored vests, and black coats, their mostly Japanese passengers either sitting impassively or taking photographs.

"The Loos House." Jane pointed at a corner building with clean lines.

Bird looked at her quizzically.

"Adolf Loos. The modernist architect. The building scandalized Viennese high society. Franz Joseph was outraged."

"No kidding. Don't see why. By the way," Bird said, as they turned into the fashionable Kohlmarkt, "what kind of name is Sweet? Wasp?"

"No, Ukrainian. Used to be Svit, but my father Americanized it. He called me Ivanka."

"No kidding. Sosenko and Kanapa were Russian, too. And Bazarov's from Odessa. You speak the language?"

"A bit. I have a terrible accent. By the way, Russians aren't—"

"So did Sosenko and Kanapa. But"—he grinned—"only when they spoke English."

"—Ukrainians." Why bother? she thought. "What about Clausen?"

"Nah," said Bird, "sounds foreign, but I think he was from Minnesota or Pennsylvania or someplace like that."

"And Bazarov?"

"Funny thing about him. Spoke perfect English. A real orator. And smooth as silk. Unlike the other three."

"So why this incredible hostility to them?"

"Look." Bird's face assumed a serious expression. "All academics are bastards. We know that. But we act like we're not. It's a kind of unwritten code. You're supposed to be a gentleman, honest and ethical and all that crap. Those three guys, I mean those four guys, they broke the code. They acted as if there were no code, as if it applied to everyone else, but not to them. Everybody hated them, not because they were sons of bitches, but because they openly acted like sons of bitches." Bird looked around him, as if trying to determine where they were. "That's where academics draw the line."

"Some line," Jane said.

"No kidding."

They joined three men and two women in the restaurant. After introductions were made, Jane could recall only that the two men in black turtlenecks were German, the third had a sweaty palm, and the two women were Russian. It took them several minutes to take their seats—someone had suggested a boy-girl arrangement, but some shuffling about had revealed that the numbers weren't right for that—but as soon as they did, Bird immediately hailed the *Herr Ober* and ordered two carafes of red and white wine along with three plates of mixed appetizers and pita bread.

"That should do, right?" he asked. "We can always get more later."

"I will just be having water," said one of the Germans. "Or maybe I order beer?"

The group fell momentarily silent, until one of the women remarked, "Those killings give me creeps."

"I wouldn't call them creeps," Sobaka laughed. "Bastards, yes. Motherfuckers, yes. But creeps, no." The table broke into laughter, and after someone said *prosit* they lifted their glasses.

"So tell me," Jane said, "why does everybody hate them?"

"Hate? No," said the man with the sweaty palm. "Despise? Yes."

"I tell you my Kanapa story, OK?" said one of the women. "One year ago, two year ago, I don't know, Kanapa he come to Moscow. He call me. 'Manya,' he say, 'Manya, meet me in bar of Metropole Hotel.' I say OK, I meet you. Why not? I go to hotel, I find bar, I see Kanapa sitting at table with half-naked woman. *Pross-tee-toot*, you know? His hand is up her skirt, her tongue is in his mouth. I say, 'Kanapa, what you want?' And you know what he say to me, that bastard? He say, 'Your *pizda*.' Many things I would do, but I never give Kanapa my *poo-see*. So I turn and go home."

"*That's* your Kanapa story?" said Ratter. "That's *all?*"

"But you not see, you stupid man? He want humiliate me. No reason. Just humiliate me. As academic? *Nyet*. As *voe-man*. You stupid man do not understand that."

"Well," countered Ratter. "I have a Clausen story that beats your Kanapa story hands down."

Jane lit a cigarette and looked at the faces around the table. Manya and the other Russian woman were whispering to each other. The two Germans were twitching nervously. The man with the sweaty palm was blowing his nose. Bird was pouring himself more wine, while Sobaka was taking a long draught from his glass.

"It was just a few months ago, actually," said Ratter, a piece of flat bread in his hand. As a drop of humus fell on his tie and slid down the purple-green paisley pattern, he raised the tip to his mouth and removed the offensive spot with his tongue.

"I was doing field research for my latest book. By the way, I'm calling it *Rereading Leather*. Good title, eh? It's a sequel to *Sites of Silk*."

Manya, sitting to Jane's right, poked her in the ribs and whispered, "Ratter is *peer-vehrt*." Jane involuntarily smiled, but remained focused on Ratter's moving lips.

"As you know, it's a study of gender construction among the so-called S and M crowd in Russia." Jane felt Manya's poke again.

"What is esenem?" she asked.

"Sadism and masochism," Jane replied coolly. Manya shrank back.

"I went to a club off Tverskaya," said Ratter. "It had been recommended to me by Tatiana Babitskaya as *the* place. As a matter of fact, Tanya and I went together. She's quite a woman, you know. It was the usual sort of thing. I mean"—at this point Ratter dragged on a cigarette—"if you've been to San Francisco and New York, nothing can really surprise you anymore." Well, thought Jane, that can only mean that a big surprise must be in store. "We went from room to room, they were whipping each other, spanking each other. You know, the usual. At the far end was a room known as Hell. There was nothing in the room, except for a hole in the middle, covered with metal bars. A group of naked men and women stood around it, and took turns pissing into the hole."

"Oh God!" cried the other Russian woman. "But why urinate in hole? They think they are in concentration camp?"

"Oh dear, no," said Ratter, "that wasn't it at all, Valya. Why they were pissing on Clausen, of course, and he seemed to be enjoying it immensely." Ratter sat back with a satisfied smirk.

"And what did you and Tanya do?" asked Bird.

"We participated," said Ratter. "Of course."

"But Clausen your friend!" cried Valya.

Ratter turned serious. "I am an anthropologist. And besides"—his smile had returned—"when in Rome...."

"Rome?" Valya looked confused. "Rome? What Rome?"

Jane shuddered. She felt Bird's heavy hand on her left knee. *What do I do now, Mike?* She crossed her right leg over her left and pressed hard. Bird's hand was trapped. Visibly distressed by this unexpected turn of events, he cleared his throat and asked if anyone had a Sosenko or Bazarov story that would top Ratter's. No one spoke up, but the two Germans rose from their chairs and, after leaving a crisp ten-Euro note on the table, said they had to go.

"Unfortunately," one of them said. "It is necessary."

"*Eine Rezeption*," the other remarked. "A Green Party *Aktion* to protect the ecology."

As they proceeded to shake everyone's hand, Jane squeezed harder, watching Bird's distress turn to embarrassment. As the Germans approached Bird, she let go of his hand. Out it sprang from under the table, knocking against Ratter's wineglass and spilling its contents on his shirt.

"What the hell!" he cried.

"So sorry," said Bird, "so very sorry. My hand must have fallen asleep."

One of the Germans seized Bird's hand and pumped it vigorously. "*Guten Abend*," he grinned. "We see you tomorrow. At our panel, *ja?*"

It was an opportune time to make her own escape, so Jane poked Manya in the ribs and suggested that the three women go to some cafe.

"These men," said Manya under her breath. "They are *deez-gahz-teeng*. Too bad only three die, no?"

Jane ordered a melange, while Manya and Valya ordered tea. The Frauenhuber was almost empty. A gray-haired woman in an olive-green hat and pearl necklace sat in one corner, sipping wine and reading a newspaper. A man in a brown suit and blue shirt was smoking a pipe. A young couple was holding hands in the booth by the window. He wore a silk ascot, white shirt, and navy blue sweater. She—a kilt, a white blouse, and delicate diamond earrings. From the nineteenth *Bezirk*, Jane thought. Vienna's rich still dressed as if the sixties had never happened.

"Is there no Sosenko story?" she asked. "Or did we break up before anyone got around to it?"

"Boring old man," said Manya. "He was blue."

"You mean drunk?" asked Jane, thinking that Manya had used the Viennese expression.

"Maybe he drink," Manya waved her hand dismissively. "I don't know. He was blue—oh, how you say *goluboy*, Valya?"

"He was homosexual," Valya said. "He like boys. Especially," she lowered her voice, "very small boys."

"You see," said Manya to Jane, "Sosenko story really not very funny."

Manya dropped two lumps of sugar into her tea, stirred it loudly, and took an all too audible sip. I wouldn't have noticed that, thought Jane. Two years ago, I wouldn't have noticed that. Valya just stared at the steaming pot and empty cup.

"Would you like me to pour you some?" asked Jane.

"*Nyet*," answered Valya. "I mean, no."

"Is something wrong?"

"I am being worried about Igor Alexandrovich."

Jane looked puzzled.

"Bazarov. Igor Alexandrovich Bazarov. Igor is first name and Alexandrovich is patronymic. After father," said Valya.

"Do you think something happened to him?"

"Where he is?" said Valya. "He supposed to meet me today. But where Igor Alexandrovich? Poof! He gone. Where he is gone?" Valya extended both her hands and opened her eyes widely. "That is why I am being worried."

"Perhaps he went back home? To the United States."

"*Eem-poe-see-bull*." This time it was Manya who spoke. "He never check out. I ask. Receptionist say he never check out. Who go home and never check out? Huh?"

"*Tochno*," said Valya triumphantly. "That is it, exactly."

"Were you supposed to meet?"

"He say he take me to Mir."

"The *Meer*? You mean the ocean?" Since when did Valya speak German?

"Ocean? What ocean?" It was Valya's turn to be puzzled. "Mir is foundation. It give him money."

"So what do you think happened?" asked Jane. "I mean, where do you think he is?"

"Maybe he is where Kanapa and Sosenko and Clausen is," Valya said solemnly. "Maybe he is being dead."

It was dark and cold, but Jane decided to walk home. She had to think, to sort out the many impressions of the day, to clear her head. Once she crossed the Ring, the streets were empty. She could hear her heels strike the sidewalk; she could hear her own breathing. And she could hear the voices, again the voices, amidst the setting sun, the cool breeze, the dark leaves. Disjointed sentences. Who is talking? They are all talking. *You never stop talking, you never ever stop talking, do you?* I spend the night in a barn. *Who? Who are you?* The sweet smell of hay, the nervousness of the horses remind me of home. I take the onion out of my pocket, peel it, and bite in. I pass the Victory of Communism collective farm. The houses are empty, the tractors stand in the field, the livestock are gone. I rummage through the pantry and find some onions and two potatoes. Pictures of Stalin adorned with embroideries hang on the walls. Near the well lies the body of a barefoot boy. I eat the potatoes and hide the onions in my pockets, for later. The wheat fields sway rhythmically, a light breeze caresses my cheeks. Burnt-out Soviet tanks line the road. Corpses, black and decomposing, lie in the grass. Crows circle above. Columns of black smoke rise beyond the trees, beyond the hills. In the distance shells explode. As I emerge from the wood, I come upon a soldier, half-dead, dying, lying in the shadow of his tank. The man sees me and, turning his head, moans, lifting his arm from what remains of his legs. Blood soaks the ground beneath him, his face is black, his tongue white. Water, he moans. I have none, I reply, but I have something better. I pull a bottle of vodka from my coat pocket, remove the cork, and pour its contents into the dying man's greedy mouth. *Spasibo*, he mutters as he falls over.

Will you never stop talking?
Will you never stop talking?
Will you never stop talking?
Will you never leave me alone?

A drunk stumbled by as Jane opened the front door to her building. She pressed the light switch and removed several items from the mailbox. She climbed the stairs, two steps at a time, to the fifth floor and entered her apartment. The cats were already waiting in the kitchen. She filled their bowls and poured herself a glass of soymilk. There were two postcards, one from Helga, who was having an absolutely *wunderbar* time in Bali, and one from Sylvie, who couldn't come to visit and was very sorry, but maybe Jane would like to come to Paris? Letters from Greenpeace and Amnesty International asked for contributions, again. And *The Economist* wondered whether Russia wasn't flexing its muscles too openly. Jane threw the mail into the trashcan and turned off the light.

Next morning Jane first made a point of telling Bristol to go to hell. Then she knocked on the ambassador's door. He was leaning back in his chair, his feet on his desk, a cup in one hand, a cigar in the other. This guy's too much, Jane thought. Was he *trying* to be the kind of American the Europeans love to hate?

"Love these Cubans," he muttered. "Only thing this country is good for. So what have you got, Sweet?"

"Seems like those three academics had a friend who's disappeared. Igor Bazarov."

"Russian?"

"No, sir, American. He's a professor, sir, like the others. They were colleagues." Jane paused. "All their friends hate them. As a matter of fact, I'd say they're happy they're dead."

"Some friends."

"I can't imagine why an academic project would get anyone killed, but that's the only thing they have in common."

"Listen, Sweet." The ambassador reached for the ashtray. "Go find that Bar-razov character."

"But sir, I'm not an operative."

"Oh, come on, Sweet," he said calmly. "Join the big boys. And besides, this could be your ticket out of here."

Or yours, she thought.

"And if I *don't* find him?" she asked.

"Then you'll live happily ever after in beautiful Vienna."

Up yours, she thought.

CHAPTER 3

▼

The screeching sound of a trolley awoke him. Bazarov dropped his legs to the floor, rubbed his aching back, and stood up from the narrow couch. As he did so, he knocked his hip against the table and heard the rattling of china. After stumbling about in the little room, he found the switch and turned on the yellow light. The ceiling lamp was a three-pronged colored wood and curled metal spider-like device that had obviously been the brainchild of Brezhnevite designers. Vika had left him breakfast on the table. Tea, a jar of sugar, a plateful of cheap sausage and crumbly cheese, butter, several slices of roughly cut black bread, and a cup filled with honey. What a wonderful woman, he thought. He scratched his belly, poured himself some tea, and crossed the room—marveling at the cacophony of colors and geometric shapes so typical of Soviet households—to enter the claustrophobic kitchen. Surrounded by cupboards and piles of pots and pans, Vilen, wrapped in a bathrobe, was seated on a stool, reading a newspaper and sipping tea from a chipped cup.

"Did you sleep well? The couch is old."

Bazarov nodded.

"Dynamo lost to Milan," said Vilen. "And our president and prime minister say that everyone will become rich after the elections." He folded the newspaper and placed it on the bench beside him. "They are fools, and they think that we are even bigger fools."

He and Vilen Titov had been childhood friends, living in the same cramped communal apartment in Odessa, sharing the same kitchen and toilet, and witnessing the same bouts of parental anger and lovemaking. They had remained close through university, even though Vilen had studied mathematics and Bazarov had decided on a career in international relations. After Bazarov had emigrated in the late seventies—having married the 85-year old Sara Moiseevna Berenstheyn, a former brigade leader and Communist Party organizer at the Glory to Lenin factory—they lost contact, but then, during the breathless days of perestroika, began corresponding. They saw each other again in 1991, when Bazarov came to Kiev for a conference on "Socialism and Sovereignty." They recognized each other immediately and resumed the close friendship that had been interrupted over a decade before.

"So tell me"—Titov finshed his tea—"why are you here?"

"I need your help, Vilen Vladimirovich."

"My help? How can I help you, my friend?"

"I need you to hide me." Bazarov paused. "And I need you to find out who is after me."

Titov smiled. He unscrewed the bottle of vodka standing in the middle of the table and filled two glasses. They threw back the hundred grams, grimaced, and slammed their glasses against the tabletop. Titov filled them again.

"You want to hide, my dear friend? Well, you are hidden. But why are you hiding?" They drank the vodka and Titov refilled the glasses.

For a moment Bazarov considered telling the truth.

"Three of my colleagues have been killed. I don't know why and I don't know who, but I think I may be next."

"Ah," said Titov thoughtfully, "but why should you be next? If my business associates got killed, I would know whether I should be next."

Bazarov understood exactly what Vilen had in mind. Having abandoned the mathematics profession in the early nineties, Titov had decided to parlay his ability to think abstractly and his connections in the state bank into *biznes*. He first began dealing in used cars, preferably German makes brought into Ukraine without the formal consent of their bourgeois owners. A crate of vodka in the trunk usually sufficed to persuade the border guards to look the other way. In the mid-nineties, when the Kiev government began privatizing state-owned industries, Titov had the money to buy up the vouchers that had been distributed to a confused populace. Most people hadn't a clue about what to do with their shares in what was euphemistically called the country's national wealth and were more than happy to sell them for hard cash. Within a year Titov had significant interests in a variety of enterprises dealing in oil and gas. His holding company, Intergaz, was registered in Cyprus, where Titov also bought himself a lavish villa overlooking the azure waters of the Mediterranean. But unlike many of the post-Soviet world's "new Russian" and "new Ukrainian" *nouveaux riches*, he stayed in the shadows, avoiding flashy clothes, ostentatious cars, and a high pro-file as a power-wielding oligarch. *Biznes* was its own reward, not unlike solving Fermat's Theorem. And besides, Titov's other commercial interests—one factory produced pirated compact disks and another transformed Uzbek poppies into high-grade cocaine—mandated a low profile. His shabby apartment in Kiev's old Podol district contributed to that image.

"Why should I be next?" said Bazarov. "A good question, my friend. I can only guess at the answer."

"So guess."

"My three colleagues and I were active in anti-Soviet organizations. I will not bother you with the names. We had thick files in the KGB. I think someone is paying us back."

"You mean the Russian secret service?"

"*Da.* It can only be them."

"But, my dear friend, they are businessmen and thieves, not killers. And why would they want to kill all four of you just now? It does not make sense."

"No it does not." Bazarov shook his head. "No it does not. But that is why I must hide and you must help me find out."

"Of course, my dear friend, of course," Titov replied. "Let us drink to our friendship." As he raised his glass, he noticed that Bazarov averted his eyes.

"Vilen!" Vika Andreevna cried as she opened the door. "I'm home."

"He's out," said Bazarov. "May I help you with those packages?"

"Vilen drinks too much," she said, looking at the half-empty bottle of vodka. "And you do, too."

As she dropped the groceries on the kitchen table, Bazarov placed his hands on her soft hips. "Igor Alexandrovich!" she cried. "Not here," she quickly added. "The table is too flimsy."

They went into the bedroom, where Bazarov pushed her on the couch. She hiked up her skirt and spread her thick legs as Bazarov dropped his pants and mounted her. The springs creaked in response to their rhythmic motion. Vika moaned.

"Do you still love me, Igorchik?" she asked, using the diminutive. Bazarov pressed his lips and said nothing. Vika moaned again.

"Or do you just love my *pizda*?"

As his groans intensified, Vika pulled away and pressed her thighs tightly together.

"Is it me or my cunt, Igorchik?"

"You, you, of course," he cried. She opened her thighs. A few quick thrusts and Bazarov became limp. He remained lying on her soft body and then jerked himself away.

"Igorchik!" she whispered.

"*Pizda*," he hissed.

"*Khuy!*" she laughed. "Prick!"

As Vika Andreevna began combing her hair, Bazarov poured himself a glass of vodka. It was warm, he noted with distaste. He walked up to her and cupped her breasts from behind.

"Stop," she said. "Vilen will be here any minute."

"I want you again."

"Later. And put your pants on."

Filatov handed the customs official his documents. She glanced at his identification card, straightened her back upon seeing who he was and, after involuntarily saluting, smiled sheepishly and returned his papers. Filatov smiled back. Old habits die hard, he thought, don't they?

"Where can I find the officer in charge?" he asked.

"*Vot on*," she said, pointing to a tall young man with rows of unfamiliar medals across his chest.

The officer had a vigorous handshake and Filatov flinched. The Ukrainian grinned. "*Izvinite*," he said. "Excuse me. If you follow me I can tell you exactly what you want."

He led the way through the crowds and opened a milky glass door. Four bored-looking women sat before a row of bright green monitors. The floor was littered with cigarette butts.

"Allochka," he said. "Bazarov, Igor Alexandrovich. Did he arrive here yesterday or today? From Vienna."

She scrolled down the screen. "*Vchera*," she said, "yesterday." She looked up. "The flight was late. Twenty minutes."

"*Dyakuyu Vam*," the officer said in Ukrainian. He then turned to Filatov. "Good luck. You have not been here for many years. I do not think you will recognize our country."

A small man in a fur hat and brown leather jacket was waiting for Filatov near the exit. He took his luggage and silently led the way to the black Mercedes parked at the curb. Filatov lit a cigarette as they drove down the highway leading from the terminal. The airport had been thoroughly modernized—thanks to a loan from the gullible Europeans—and billboards advertising Western products now lined the road, but otherwise Ukraine seemed no different from what it had been when he had last been here, in Soviet times. The rickety bus shelters, the massive housing blocks, the ubiquitous peasant women with pails of berries. Blue and yellow, the colors of independent Ukraine's flag, had replaced the Soviet red, but they seemed to have the exact same function—to remind people that they should expect little of substance from the regime. Russia was no different. After all those years of so-called reform, most Russians still lived in the nineteenth century and only Moscow looked like a real city.

The Mercedes crossed the Dniepr and turned right onto the road that wound its way through the wooded hills separating the river from the city. A few minutes later they drove past the presidential palace and the Parliament—the engraving of the hammer and sickle still adorned the top of the building—down a steep hill and, after negotiating several narrow turns, stopped in front of what used to be the Hotel Moskva, a flat-faced ugly structure overlooking what used to be Lenin Square. The Moskva had traditionally served as a meeting place for spies, thieves, and smugglers. Just the place to track down Bazarov and let him know that his killer is on his trail.

The ill-lit lobby reeked of cheap tobacco. Four men in black leather jackets and jeans were arguing near the currency exchange window. A portrait of the Ukrainian president—his mouth fixed in a stupid grin—hung on the wall behind the reception desk. The thickset woman gave Filatov a poorly printed form and asked for his signature. After handing him his key, she pointedly asked him if he needed anything. Filatov answered no and proceeded to the elevator. Just before the door closed, a bleach blonde with purple lipstick and a leather miniskirt stepped in and also asked him if he needed anything.

"*Nyet*," he answered.

"Too bad," she said on her way out. "Perhaps later."

After taking a quick shower—the drain was clogged, so the water gathered around his ankles as he soaped his body with the irregularly hewn chunk placed on the bathroom sink—Filatov made a phone call and, his hair still wet, left his room. The elevator stopped on the mezzanine, and three tall men with shaven heads swaggered inside. Filatov stepped back into a corner. One of them pressed the fifth-floor button and cursed after the elevator resumed its descent. As Filatov pushed past them to exit, they laughed. "Let the old man through," one said.

Kostenko was sitting at the far end of the bar, a glass of cognac before him. Gold chains adorned his neck and wrists.

"*Nu?*" he asked.

"Igor Alexandrovich Bazarov," said Filatov. He offered Kostenko a Marlboro and took one himself.

"Who is he?"

"An American, an émigré. A professor."

"Where is he?"

"Here."

"Why do you want him?"

"Here's his photograph," said Filatov. "Find him."

Filatov paused at the top of the stairs leading down to Independence Square. He noted the spot where the large statue of Lenin used to stand. Below was Kiev's main boulevard, the Khreshchatyk. The buildings that lined it had for the most part been constructed after the Great Patriotic War in unmistakably Stalinist wedding-cake style. Workers and peasants would march down it, banners and spirits raised, on May Day, bearing witness to the Party's wise leadership. Filatov smiled. Now the Khreshchatyk was full of cars and pedestrians. Obolon beer stands were located on every block. At least the old Sovpress newspaper kiosks were still there, manned by invisible babushkas with never enough change.

Filatov descended into the underground passage. Its walls were thick with unevenly pasted posters, some torn, others in fading colors, enjoining voters to support various candidates. Ramshackle shops were selling videocassettes, compact disks, tapes, and cheap jewelry. Filatov stopped to listen to some fanatic dressed in faux Cossack attire—Turkish-style trousers, an embroidered shirt, an incongruous orange scarf, and an enormous fur hat—denouncing Russian imperialism. Filatov could not resist a chuckle. That had been an easy job—arranging for that ridiculous nationalist's removal back in 1982. Valentin Ostapenko, a wiry man with thick eyebrows and protruding cheekbones, a mini-Führer who believed it was his mission to rally the oppressed Ukrainian masses against the Russian imperialists. He wrote bad poetry, organized something called the Anti-Imperialist Front of the Ukrainian Working People—which consisted of him, his wife, his two mistresses, and three drinking buddies, two of whom were KGB informants reporting to Filatov—and threatened to immolate himself during the May Day parade in Kiev. Well, we beat him to the punch. As he was driving to the capital city in his ancient Zaporozhets, poor Ostapenko appears to have had too much to drink and, despite the best efforts of the driver in the oncoming truck, smashed right into it. His car immediately burst into flames, the driver mysteriously disappeared, and the Anti-Imperialist Front crumbled under the shock. The nationalists were outraged, claiming murder and producing a slew of samizdat denunciations, but few people read them and even fewer passed them on, and within two months Ostapenko had become a non-person.

Nothing was easier than eliminating intellectuals and pseudo-intellectuals like Ostapenko. They lived in their rooms, they lived at their typewriters. Pens and pencils and white sheets of paper were their whole world. Compared to the lives we led, theirs were a joke. The comrades in the underground lived alone, but they fought for the world. These writers claimed to be living for the world, but could not bear their alone-ness. They needed publicity, newspapers, magazine articles, interviews, lights. They were cowards. You had only to praise their work, praise their courage, and they would trust you. Your poetry is so bold. Your essays are so daring. Your latest novel is a masterpiece of critical thinking. They loved it. They loved being told how bold, how critical they were. The secret police are after you, he would say. How do you know? I saw them following you, he would reply. They were wearing different coats, and they changed personnel every two blocks, but they followed you all the way there and back. How flattered they would be when he told them such things. And how frightened. But their sense of self-importance always proved greater than their fear. I am not afraid of those thugs, they would say, truth is on my side. So why are you sweating? Why do you go out only after dark? Why do you avoid your favorite cafes and restaurants? Why do you slink along the sides of the streets like mangy dogs?

Enough, Filatov thought. He climbed the stairs near the Main Post Office, went inside, made a phone call, and then turned left into the narrow streets of old Kiev. When he found the building he was looking for, he took the graffiti-scarred elevator to the sixth floor—the familiar smell of cooking oil and urine was almost reassuring—and knocked three times on the door at the far end of the corridor. The door opened a centimeter or two. A raspy voice said, "Do you want to come in from the snow?" and Filatov answered, "Only from the rain"—the exchange of passwords struck him as absurd—and he entered a dark apartment with peeling wallpaper and worn-out linoleum.

"*Privet, tovarishch,*" said the little man who had opened the door. "Greetings, comrade."

They sat on a sagging couch opposite a desk, computer, and mounds of paper. The little man produced a half-empty bottle of Armenian brandy and poured two glasses.

"Anatoly Sergeevich," he began, "how may I serve you?" The little man had been in the employ of the KGB and was still retained as an informant by the Russian FSB. His information was never spectacular, but he was reliable and could be counted on to do Filatov's bidding.

"Igor Alexandrovich Bazarov," he said. "I am looking for him. He is here. In Kiev." Filatov took a sip of the brandy. "He arrived yesterday from Vienna."

"Bazarov?" said the little man. "That is his real name?" He looked at Filatov expectantly. "Of course that is his real name. One second, just one second. Hmm, Bazarov, Bazarov, Bazarov. The name rings a bell." He stood up from the couch and walked to the file cabinet. "One second, I may have something on him." He opened a drawer and ran his fingers across the tops of dog-eared files. "Aha!" he cried. "Here it is."

"Bazarov, Igor Alexandrovich," he began reading. "Born 1945 in Odessa, nationality—Russian, father, Russian, a longshoreman, mother, Belorussian, a worker in the Glory to Lenin watch factory. Education—Institute of International Relations. You know what that means, of course. Speaks English, French, Polish, and German. Outstanding student, member of the Komsomol, wrote a good thesis, member of the Party, and so on and so on. Married a Jew—she could have been his grandmother—emigrated to the United States in 1979—"

"You are wasting my time," said Filatov. "I know all this already."

"Ah, but there is one more thing here." The little man was unruffled. "Did you know that your Bazarov was an informant while at the Institute? His code name was *Chas*, the Ukrainian word for time. Apparently because he never wasted any. His reports should be at Vladimirskaya. That's just a few—"

"I know." The headquarters of the Ukrainian security service were in the building formerly occupied by the local KGB, several blocks away in what the Ukrainians insisted on calling Volodymyrska Street. Filatov finished the brandy.

"If I learn anything about this Bazarov," the little man said, "where can I reach you?"

"The Moskva."

"Oh, but of course. It is now called something else. Did you know?"

The little man fell silent. Poor creature, thought Filatov. You are as pathetic as your files and codes. A relic of the past. Isn't that what we used to call vestiges of bourgeois behavior? You are a relic of the past, little man. You are a vestige of proletarian behavior. Filatov sighed as he rose from the chair. The little man caught his glance as he did so.

"I have other files," he said. "Some of them are quite interesting, possibly even valuable."

You stupid little man, thought Filatov. Have you no shame?

"Such as mine?"

"Times are hard. It is impossible to live."

"You are right," Filatov said softly. "You are quite right. It is impossible for you to live."

A few seconds later, he lifted the limp corpse and placed it gently on the bed. His neck broken, the little man's head slid off the pillow and lodged against his shoulder. Filatov took off his shoes and covered him with a blanket. *Rest in peace, you stupid little man.*

He opened the cabinet and found his file. What it contained was utterly routine. A list of his assignments in the Ukrainian SSR, basic biographical data, even a copy of a report he had written in the eighties. *The stupid little man had been bluffing. And I fell for it, like an amateur. This was a bad sign. I do not make mistakes; I do not make stupid mistakes. It is this country. It unnerves me. It throws me off balance.*

Filatov opened the bedroom window and disconnected the phone. He pulled the body off the bed, emptied the man's pockets, and scattered some papers on the floor. After he wiped the cabinet, glass, and armrests for fingerprints, Filatov locked the front door, placed the key under the doormat, and descended the staircase. *I have sinned,* he thought, *this time I have sinned—grievously, unnecessarily, mortally.*

Filatov passed a white-haired woman carrying several loaves of bread and a bottle of milk on her way upstairs. She stopped on the landing above him, and he could hear her labored breathing. Once outside, he walked up the hill toward St. Sophia Square. The magnificent eleventh-century cathedral had recently been renovated. Craggy, toothless old women, all dressed in black, crowded the entrance with their gnarled hands outstretched. He gave each one a dollar and watched them hide the money in the thick folds of their clothes. He decided to go inside. The faded frescoes that adorned the undulating walls had always mesmerized him. Their blurred quality conveyed both transience and some deeper, barely visible, reality. *Dima,* he thought, would call it "wallness." Filatov stopped for a few minutes and tried to focus his eyes on the indistinct lines. On the way out he almost crossed himself. *How odd,* he thought, *but how appropriate.*

After he reemerged into the sunlight he nodded to the black women and, despite the street signs that proclaimed Volodymyrska, turned down Vladimirskaya. The Soviet Ukrainian KGB had a deserved reputation for being especially assiduous, always ready to accept and follow Moscow's orders, always willing to exert just a bit more effort and apply just a bit more force. Ukraine's dissidents had no chance. Notwithstanding their inability to pronounce the hard Russian "g," the Ukrainian chekists had been good and reliable comrades. Unlike some other Ukrainians, especially those with the recently acquired fetish for the color orange, they had not let the illusion of independence go to their heads—or at least not entirely.

"This is somewhat unusual," said Colonel Shevchenko, "but we are always happy to help our Russian colleagues and friends. After all, we are all Slavs."

Shevchenko's office, located on the second floor of the Ukrainian security service, faced Vladimirskaya Street and was just above the tree line. It was brightly lit, but the ceiling and walls needed painting. Positioned above his desk was a small portrait of the doltish Ukrainian president. Filatov could see that a larger frame used to occupy that space. He wondered where Shevchenko had stashed the portrait of Lenin.

"*Spasibo*," Filatov said in Russian. "Someday, Taras Grigorovich, I will return the favor."

Shevchenko smiled. "Something to drink?" he asked, and without waiting for a reply pulled a bottle of French cognac from a desk drawer. "Ararat is no longer any good, and ours is undrinkable." He handed Filatov a thick file consisting of handwritten pages. "Bazarov's reports. He was quite a useful asset. Take your time. I'll be back in a minute."

Filatov skimmed through the pages. He had seen such reports countless times, and these differed in no way from the standard material produced by all informants. Subject X left the house wearing a dark coat and blue hat. Subject X walked slowly down such-and-such street. Subject X was carrying a briefcase. Subject X spoke on the telephone. Subject X was working on a new story entitled something or other. Subject X, subject Y, subject Z. It was always the same. The details never varied, because there was nothing to write about. The lives and exploits of fakes and cowards could not be interesting. X, Y, and Z were letters of the alphabet, not people.

What *was* interesting was Bazarov's reputation for efficiency—it dawned upon Filatov that the Russian word for clock, *chasy*, was obviously related to the Ukrainian word for time, *chas*—and his later emigration. There were always a few informants who truly believed in what they were being paid to do, but it was hard to imagine that Bazarov's efficiency was the product of zeal. There had to be another angle, obviously one involving monetary gain. The other question was whether he continued working as an informant in the United States.

Shevchenko returned, adjusting his zipper. "Have you found anything of interest?"

"The usual," Filatov replied. "But tell me. Why do you think Bazarov was such"—he seemed to search for the right word—"an ideal informant?"

"It is obvious. He believed."

"In communism?" Filatov shook his head. "In himself."

Shevchenko said nothing.

"But if so, then what was he up to?"

Again Shevchenko remained silent.

"He was in it for profit," Filatov answered his own question. "But since his only commodity was information, then that was obviously what he was selling. To you."

"Yes," Shevchenko broke his silence with a smile, "to us."

"And to them." Filatov looked at Shevchenko.

"And to them."

"So he took you—*us*—for a ride."

"In a manner of speaking."

"And did Bazarov stay on your payroll in New York?"

"What does the file say?" Shevchenko avoided Filatov's gaze.

"The file says nothing."

"Then the answer must obviously be no."

Filatov closed the file. "Obviously."

He could not resist contemplating the irony. Shevchenko Boulevard, named after Ukraine's national poet, was just a few blocks away from the office of Shevchenko the ex-persecutor of national poets. Filatov stopped to look at the University, painted red, to his right. To his left stood the yellow building that once housed the Institute of International Relations, where Bazarov had studied back in the sixties. The Institute produced international relations specialists for a country—Soviet Ukraine—that had no international relations to speak of. Many of its graduates joined the KGB; most had to report to the KGB. Some had even been his comrades-in-arms in Vienna and Berlin. Filatov turned down the boulevard. The traffic, though not quite up to Moscow's standards, was impressive—a far cry from the old Soviet days when a few battered Zhigulis and shiny black Volgas dominated the streets. But the trucks hadn't changed. They still resembled poorly constructed toys that seemed to move in all directions at once.

At the foot of the boulevard, where it crossed the Khreshchatyk, Filatov was surprised to see that the bronze statue of Lenin still stood. Someone had even left a bouquet of red carnations at the great man's feet. The corner building, which had once been home to the Donbas cafe—a dingy place frequented by students and informants—now housed a supermarket. A guard carrying a submachine gun stood at the entrance. Kiev *had* changed, as everything in the former Soviet Union had changed. But why should that surprise me? It does not. It only saddens me. It was like looking at the frescoes in the Sophia Cathedral: the past was blurred, indistinct, receding into forgetfulness, into oblivion. Fortunately, the Bessarabian Market across the Khreshchatyk had not changed since tsarist times. The round peasant faces, the alarmingly ruddy cheeks, the thick slabs of fat, the piles of mushrooms, the dark-haired Armenian smugglers, the stacks of caviar tins, the bottles of vodka. Filatov plowed through the crowds and exited at the back. He looked at his watch, realized that he had to be back at the hotel in twenty minutes, and walked hurriedly up the Khreshchatyk. It was full of people, some strolling arm in arm, others seemingly in a hurry. It was that old Soviet habit of rushing. You had all the time in the world, but the constant shortages meant always being on the lookout for *defitsitnye* products. Always carrying more cash than you could possibly need, except that you knew that it was perfectly possible that you'd need just that much cash.

As agreed, Kostenko was waiting in the hotel bar. Filatov sidled up to him and placed his arm around his shoulders. He squeezed tightly. "So," he said, "what do you have for me?"

"Bazarov is staying at the home of Vilen Vladimirovich Titov," Kostenko answered. "Titov is a good man, one of us. But he is also an old friend of Bazarov." Kostenko curled his lip. "Bazarov used to screw Titov's wife. Before they got married. Maybe he's still screwing her. Who knows?

"Here's the address," he added.

"Tell Titov to take his wife out to a late dinner tomorrow."

Kostenko nodded and downed his drink.

"Wait," said Filatov, "I wanted to ask you something."

"What?"

"What did you do before?"

"Before all this"—Kostenko paused—"independence?"

"*Da.*"

Kostenko laughed. "I was a thief."

"And now you are a businessman."

"But that is only half the irony," retorted Kostenko. "The other half is that *you* are my partner."

Exhausted by the day's wanderings, Filatov decided on dinner at the Moskva. The restaurant was full, mostly men, usually two to a table, huddled over in whispered conversations. The waiter directed him to a table near a grimy window. The tablecloth was stained, and a plastic flower in a small vase stood forlornly next to a jar filled with bent toothpicks. There was no need to look at the menu. He ordered a Jubilee salad, borscht, and chicken Kiev, along with a beer for starters and a bottle of vodka to accompany the meal. Filatov lit a cigarette and leaned back in his chair. Kostenko was a good man. They had met once before and he had struck him as tough and reliable, qualities that were indispensable in this business. Everyone he knew praised him. Titov he had never met, just heard of. A self-made man, an intellectual turned biznesman, a post-Soviet success story, a capitalist Stakhanov. He would know why Kostenko asked him to leave home, and he would know not to ask why. Would he warn Bazarov? No, not with all that money on the line. Filatov pushed away the plate and finished the rest of the vodka.

He climbed the stairs to his room and, without removing his shoes, threw himself into an easy chair. He turned on the television. The news anchor, a severe-looking young woman with short dark hair, was talking of the president's trip, the Parliament's debates, the grain harvest, and the prime minister's popularity and successful presidential campaign. A commercial, for toothpaste, interrupted the program. Then the anchor returned with news of a conference in Kiev, a riot in Pakistan, a mine explosion in the Donbas, and a helicopter crash in the Crimea. A series of images: children going to school, torrential rain in the mountains, angry workers waving their fists, a dull bureaucrat. Refugees, terrified faces, drunken faces. Another commercial, this time for a soft drink. Filatov lifted one leg and draped it over the other.

This was all too familiar. The seventies and eighties, when Soviet power entered the "era of stagnation," when everyone sensed something was very wrong. He recalled the drunks lining the sidewalks, sprawled in the doorways, empty bottles of cheap liquor next to them, their clothes stained, their crotches wet, their faces unshaved. They swayed, occasionally stopping, turning, extending a hand, and then resumed their swaying. Sometimes they fell, lying there like a crumpled mass of dirty clothes. Sometimes they'd shout crazy senseless things. But mostly they just swayed, going somewhere, going nowhere—just like the Soviet Union. The drug addicts came later, standing in doorways, smoking, shifting their weight from foot to foot, wiggling their heads to set their hair free.

Filatov opened his eyes. The television was still playing. He could tell from the intonation of the voices—all declamatory and heroic—that it was a Soviet war film. The fascists always came close to winning, they would torture us, they would beat us, but in the end we would win. He watched the heroic Soviet troops arrive in tanks. An official delegation awaits them in the main square. Peasants wave red flags. Girls wearing embroidered shirts carry bread and salt. The patriarchal general approaches the townsfolk and shakes hands with the mayor. He speaks lovingly to the crowd, calling them comrades. The people cheer. Another round of commercials. Then, the next scene. A boy is asleep. A knock on the window awakes him. He peers out and catches the outlines of a familiar figure motioning him to come outside. He quietly opens the door. Everyone is still asleep. The cold air slaps him in the face. What do you want? he asks. We need your help. A district commander has to be taken through the forest. We are expecting an attack tomorrow. He pulls on his trousers and jacket and follows his comrade. The commander is dressed in a Soviet army uniform. Long live Stalin, he says. They walk silently through the woods, cross a moonlit field, and approach a barn. Several men with machine guns step out of the shadows and exchange signals. The boy, frightened but proud, runs home.

Uneasy at what he had just seen, Filatov lay down on the bed. I am no longer a boy, hiding, running. I am a man. Like my father, who died for what he believed. Like him, I joined the KGB to fight the enemies of communism. But we lost and they won, and now communism is dead and I am a whiskey priest and a hit man for the mafiya. The enemies of communism deserved to die. The enemies—the *real* enemies—of the mafiya might also deserve to die. And killing both was somehow a privilege, an honor, and even a challenge. But the miserable Kanapa? And the equally pathetic Clausen and Sosenko? And that wretch, Bazarov? They were unworthy enemies and to pursue and kill them was almost like insulting yourself. And killing the little man could not be justified by any morality. Is this what I have become? A miserable hack, a cheap intellectual out for a quick buck, a corrupt cop?

Old man Gerasimenko had moral fiber. He had no ideology and no vision of the future, but he had a code of honor and he believed in what he did. And his many years in Soviet prisons testified to the firmness of those beliefs. Gerasimenko never betrayed a comrade, and he always provided for the wives and children of dead friends. His crime family shared Gerasimenko's moral system. Sometimes it needed executioners and it was willing to pay them large amounts of money to get the job done quietly and efficiently. When they approached Filatov, he had unhesitatingly said yes. When they said they'd pay him well, he had just as quickly said no. The old man didn't trust him at first: only psychopaths kill for free and there was no room in the organization for madmen. It took a long meeting and several bottles of vodka for Filatov to persuade him that his motives were pure. He would kill because the mafiya was a fallen church; he would kill as a whiskey priest struggling to save his soul; he would kill to save the world. But you'll be killing my competition, Gerasimenko had said. They're neither saints, nor sinners—just bastards who stole my money or muscled in on my territory. You can believe what you like, Filatov had answered, let me believe what I like. By the time they finished the fourth bottle, they had become friends. Do you believe in God? Gerasimenko had asked him, I do not. I do, Filatov had said, I could not imagine my life without God. But it is against God's law to kill, Gerasimenko had said. Not against my God's, Filatov had replied, my God is cruel, merciless, and just. Then your God is not my God, Gerasimenko had said.

Filatov now saw that his conversation with Gerasimenko had been pure pretence. I have no idea who my God is. I know only that I do not kill for enjoyment or for profit. Killing used to be a sacramental rite. Now it is my only hold on life. It makes this life bearable, tolerable, indeed possible. At the same time, killing has become pointless. An end in itself on the one hand. Neither a means to an end nor an end on the other. Filatov laughed. Is this what we meant by the dialectic?

Filatov fell into a deep but anxious sleep. He dreamt he was a miner. Blackness engulfed him. The screeching of the cars, the flickering of the lights, the nervous laughter of the other workers. He fidgeted in his seat. The air became colder and damper. They clambered out of the cars, and each proceeded to his corner of the mine. He crawled along the rocks. His chest was hot with sweat; his back felt cold. The candle flickered indifferently. The damp coal pressed in on him, its wet blackness enveloped him, resisting his blows, resisting his attempts to set himself free. The thud of the hammer, the rattling chain, the flickering lamp, the drip-drip-drip of water. Tears flowed down his blackened cheeks and into his mouth. He spat, wiping his brow with the back of his left hand, pounding at the rock with his right. The light flickered, a semaphore. He took a deep breath of foul air. The flame danced in the darkness, casting strange shapes onto the sides of the pit. He heard voices in the distance, but they quickly subsided. The rock was all there was to listen to again. He took the pick and resumed the conversation.

Filatov awoke with a start, his shirt wet, his heart pounding. The news program was over. The Ukrainian flag was fluttering in the wind; some anthem—but not the Soviet anthem—was playing. He fell back into the damp pillow with a groan.

The collapse of the Soviet Union had come almost as a relief to him. When you lose your faith, when heaven no longer seems possible, then the end of the world is nothing but the external manifestation of an internal condition. The end of communism meant that he could leave the priesthood. And do what? As he quickly realized, there was nothing for him to do. Other agents, especially those who had been posted abroad, had started businesses or managed to insinuate themselves into the political elite. Soon they were driving Western cars, sporting diamond rings and young women, and representing Russia in the West. See how western we are? they seemed to be saying. We are materialists and we care about nothing—just like you. So invest in Mother Russia. Better still, invest in us. Even better, give us the money and we'll invest for you. The European and American suckers fell over one another in their attempts to make millions while building a democratic Russia. Most lost their shirts in the process. Perhaps there *was* a God?

Business was not for him. He saw that immediately. Playing at democracy and kissing the West's ass was also not for him. Old habits did die hard. He may have become a whiskey priest, and God may have abandoned him, but the West was still the devil. And retirement was out of the question. So he stayed on in the revamped KGB. Now the Federal Security Service, the FSB offered him a comfortable sinecure. Assigned to a counterintelligence unit and informed that democratic Russia abjures all forms of violence, Filatov quickly became the kind of bureaucrat he so desperately despised. No, he corrected himself, he almost became that kind of bureaucrat. Thank God, he was given the opportunity to join a different church. Gerasimenko's, unfortunately, promised not salvation, only limbo.

Filatov turned off the television. It was unbearably hot in the room. He took the tiny elevator to the ground floor and walked into the darkly lit bar. The bleach blonde with purple lipstick and the leather miniskirt was sitting on one of the stools. He placed himself next to her and ordered two vodkas.

"I need something," he said. She smiled sadly in return.

CHAPTER 4

▼

Jane was beginning to hate—no, *despise*—the assignment. When she joined the State Department over a decade ago, they had tempted her with stories of crisis management, peacekeeping, all-night negotiations, hot lines, international terrorism. But this—tracking down slovenly professors who, from all that she had heard so far, were as one-dimensionally nasty as they were one-dimensionally petty—this was not what she had expected from a glorious career in the Foreign Service. Two years of working as cultural attaché in Vienna should have prepared her for the disappointment. The Austrian capital, officially equidistant from both East and West for forty-five years, had long since stopped being a center of espionage. There was still some drug smuggling, and much of the illicit trade in women went through Vienna, and yes, the place abounded with illegal immigrants and refugees from every possible godforsaken place, but that made it little different from, or more interesting or more exciting than, any number of other central European cities, such as Budapest, Bratislava, Warsaw, or Berlin. Hell, even in Zagreb there had been fighting, war criminals, ethnic cleansing. All terrible things, true, but that's what diplomats were supposed to deal with. Not investigate a bunch of creeps with overworked sexual imaginations and bulges in their pants. Of course, she wasn't a front-line diplomat, she had never been a front-line diplomat, and she would never be a front-line diplomat. She was an analyst and a cultural attaché, because they didn't trust her to be more than an analyst and a cultural attaché. Worse, she didn't trust herself to be more than that. Tracking down creeps—that's about all I *can* do. Worst of all, she had a nagging suspicion that the ambassador had something up his sleeve. Why assign me to this stupid case? Because I'm expendable, that's why. Because I was pushed through the cracks. Because if I succeed—whatever that means—he comes out looking like a tough diplomat and enlightened promoter of sexual equality. Then I'm his ticket out of here. And if I don't succeed—well, she *was* pushed through the cracks, wasn't she? Or am I just being paranoid?

Manya and Valya had told her that the Mir Foundation was in a side street near St. Stephen's. Mir, as Valya referred to it, had been established by Pyotr Mironov, a millionaire-turned-philanthropist who wanted to be known as Russia's answer to Bill Gates. *Mir* was also the Russian word for both world and peace, which possibly hinted at the size of Mironov's megalomania. He was certainly a worthy competitor for the richest man in the world. Jane laughed when she realized that *mir* was also Ukrainian for peace, while her own name, *svit*, was the Ukrainian word for world. I have, she decided, been fated for this assignment. Why resist anymore?

The foundation was housed in a turn-of-the-century building, one of the many extravagant structures that had been erected for the *haute bourgeoisie* in the heyday of Austria-Hungary. The hallway was lined with marble columns, the floor was tiled. A delicately embroidered, if somewhat unsteady looking elevator took her to the fourth floor. A small plaque, with gold engraving, announced *Die Mir Foundation*. She rang the doorbell, pushed open the heavy door, and found herself in a gaudily decorated reception area. Brass samovars had been converted into lamps, some stood on the side tables, others were affixed to the maroon walls. It was wallpaper, she realized with some horror, maroon-colored wallpaper. In the middle of the room, seated behind a glass table with one white telephone, was a blonde clad in a tight-fitting blouse and a miniskirt. She uncrossed her legs at the sight of Jane.

"*Bitte?*" The blonde smiled sweetly. With her thick Slavic accent, she pronounced the word *bee-teh*.

"*Sprechen Sie Englisch?*"

"Yes," Jane heard with relief.

"My name is Jane Sweet. I'm the cultural attaché at the United States Embassy. May I see the director?"

"Who asks?"

"I just told you. My name is Jane Sweet—"

"—and you are cultural attaché at American embassy." The blonde smiled. "Please have seat."

She rose from her geometrically designed chair—either a Wiener Werkstätte original, in which case it cost thousands, or a very clever knock-off—pulled gently at her skirt, paused to run her hands down her bottom, and walked into the room behind her. An amazing performance, Jane thought. She is cool and I am nervous. One minute later, the door opened and a rotund man in a light gray suit, beige shirt, dark gray tie, and beige loafers emerged, his right hand extended, his left stroking his ear.

He smiled, kissed Jane's outstretched hand, and bowed. "Virsky," he said, "Mikhail Virsky. Director of Mir Foundation in Vienna. Please come into office, Madame." He turned on his heels and walked back inside.

The blonde sat slumped in a red leather easy chair, her long white legs extending languorously into the center of the room. Virsky pointed to the chair opposite her and sat down behind his desk. Jane almost disappeared in the soft folds of the chair. As she looked up, she realized that Virsky was smarter than she had thought. If she looked at Virsky, she'd have to face the bright window behind him. If she looked away, she'd have to deal with the erotomania of the blonde.

"How can I be helping you, Madame?"

Jane decided to shield her eyes from the sun and talk in his direction.

"I am doing a survey of funding opportunities in Europe for American scholars. It's a service the embassy provides. And since the Mir Foundation is one of the largest in Vienna, I thought I'd drop by. Perhaps you can tell me more about what you do."

"With pleasure, with very greatest pleasure," Virsky said. "Masha," he turned to the blonde, "get for us something to drink. Maybe Crimean *shampanskoye?*"

Jane surveyed the room. Glossy brochures and what seemed like application forms lay on the coffee table. The bookshelves contained mostly Russian volumes. Three tall metal file cabinets stood in a corner. Two windows looked out onto a courtyard. The spires of St. Stephen's Cathedral were slightly visible from the window on the left. Masha returned with a tray. She handed Virsky and Jane their glasses and sat down with her own. Once again she crossed and uncrossed her legs with what seemed to Jane to be deliberate slowness.

"Where begin?" said Virsky. "I start with Mr. Mironov, who is great man, great Russian, great patriot, great philanthropist. I am honored being his loyal servant." He waited for the effect of those words to sink in.

"*Mees-ter* Mironov is millionaire and, like great millionaires of America, wants to help Russia, Russian people. You see," he added almost as an aside, "Mr. Mironov has very big and very kind heart. I know.

"Foundation is result of Mr. Mironov's dream." Virsky lapsed into grammatically correct officialese. "We were established four years ago to provide technical assistance for the construction of democracy, civil society, and the market economy in Russia. We have been very successful. Russian scientists and American scientists are building institutions in the wake of the terrible legacy of Communist totalitarianism." He paused. "It will be long struggle, but we are being confident. We must have to begin somewhere." Virsky stopped and lit a cigarette. Then he took a sip of the champagne.

"That's wonderful," Jane murmured. "Could you tell me how large your endowment is?"

"One billion dollars. American, of course. We distribute over one hundred million American dollars every year. It's not—how you say?—nuts."

"I understand that four Americans won a grant from you, Professors Bazarov, Kanapa—"

"Tragic, very tragic." Virsky shook his head. "Most excellent scholars with most excellent ideas. They love Russia. They want to help Russia. They die for Russia."

"But Professor Bazarov is, I believe, still alive," interjected Jane. "Why do you say they died for Russia?"

"I mean other three," said Virsky. "*They* die for Russia." He smiled apologetically.

"Would it be possible to see their grant proposal? If it's not confidential. Just to see what they were working on?"

Virsky shook his head. "My apologies, my most sincerest apologies. All proposals confidential. You understand. But you can read abstract. Is there, in brochure." He turned to the blonde. "Mashenka, give Madame Sweet brochure. You can keep it, of course. More champagne?

"If no more questions, please allow me excuse myself. I have important appointment at Ministry of Education. Minister is old friend—friend of me and friend of Russia. I love him, you know?" Virsky gave Jane his broadest smile. "Here for you is Mir Foundation pin—souvenir. And please call when you want. I and Masha always happy help you, yes Mashenka?" The blonde uncrossed her legs.

Go to hell, Mashenka.

Jane returned to the embassy. Bristol was away, probably at lunch, so she sat down at her desk and began reading the brochure. The glossy cover, attractive layout, and appealing typeface immediately struck her. The foundation's Vienna office may have been bizarrely decorated, but its propaganda was professional. These guys clearly knew the ways of the West. The front cover had images of serious-looking men and women—sitting or standing near computers, test tubes, and other paraphernalia supposed to convey modernity—superimposed on a map of eastern Europe. The title read "The Mir Foundation: Bringing Peace to the World." Not bad. The first page consisted of greetings from and a color photograph of the great philanthropist himself. The next two pages were devoted to him and the foundation. There followed some forty pages of project abstracts. The topics ranged from small arms proliferation to nuclear weapons control to "building civil society"—as opposed to *un*civil society?—to building nations, states, and markets. Seems like academics are desperately eager to build. And to whose benefit? From what she knew of the Soviet successor states, they were pretty dismal places to live in. The vast majority of people lived in abject poverty, and only a tiny percentage lived well—that is to say, very well. Who needed markets, nations, states, and civil societies, when simple survival was on the line?

She finally found what she was looking for—the abstract written by Bazarov and his friends. Unlike all the other projects—which received money in the fifty-thousand range—this one was funded for the incredibly large sum of ten million dollars. Jane shook her head in disbelief. After reading the abstract, she closed her eyes for several seconds and then turned in the direction of Bristol's desk. The jerk was there.

"Bristol," she said, "you've got a Ph.D. in something, don't you?"

"Yeah, in political fucking science, if you can believe it."

"Do me a favor, Bristol. Read this. Tell me what you think." She pointed to the paragraph circled in red. Bristol took the brochure and leaned back in his chair. After a few minutes he looked up.

"Bullshit," he said. "Complete and total crap. What is this, Jane?"

"What do you mean—bullshit?"

"Bullshit is bullshit. It's just pretty words, no substance. These guys are running a bunch of seminars—to empower women and build civil society? Give me a break, Jane, that's just fucking bullshit. And they're getting a cool ten for that? Give me a fucking break."

"So why did they get it?"

"How do I know? The academic mafia, I guess. It's all corrupt, you know, all these fucking academics running around looking for fucking grants to save fucking Russia. They're really out to save their own fucking selves." Bristol paused, and then pointed to the title on the brochure.

"I mean, look, Jane. Look at this title: Bringing fucking peace to the fucking world. Did you ever see a bigger load of crap? But that's the way these outfits function. They have money to spend, they haven't a clue how, and then the fucking academics come along and say, 'Hey, just it give to us and we'll bring some fucking peace to the fucking world. How about it?' And the foundation boys and girls say, 'Great. Let's bring some fucking peace to the fucking world.' Then they write about what they're doing in glossy brochures, spend a ton of money on conferences nobody needs, drink a lot of wine, and the poor people of the world remain just as poor as they were. It's a scam."

"Illegal?"

"Oh, no, perfectly legal, but perfectly unethical and perfectly corrupt. But you should know that, Jane. You *are* Russian."

"So where does all this money go?"

"Who knows? Hotels, food, travel, honoraria."

"But ten million for five years? That's two million a year? What are they doing? Inviting all of Ukraine and putting them up in the Sacher?"

"Not all of Russia, just—how does the abstract put it?—the 'leading women activists'. Who knows? Maybe it's their girlfriends."

Jane sat on the bench at the top of the Strudelhofstiege, unwrapped her *Wurstbrot*, and surveyed the slanted rooftops before her. It had taken a while, but Vienna had insinuated itself into her *Seele*, her soul. The city that tourists visited was atrocious. Hers was the Wien of hidden courtyards, mysterious passageways, onion-shaped spires, yellow ochres and venetian reds, peeling plaster, and cobblestone streets—the Vienna of the second, fifth, sixth, seventh, and eighth districts, the Vienna of long-haired *Alternativler*, of Turkish storeowners, of drug addicts, of whores. There was none of that in her native Long Island. She had escaped that antiseptic environment at the age of eighteen, leaving for college in Boston and determined never to return. And she had not. A Master's in English from Columbia, followed by a string of uninteresting jobs—in publishing, in business—had followed, until, having finally overcome her scruples about working for a government that had implicated America in a stupid war in Vietnam, she had decided to try for a job with the Central Intelligence Agency—the Company, the Agency, the core of the intelligence community, a sprawling white compound in a sylvan setting just outside Washington that looked like someplace in Long Island. And why not? If you're going to join the system, you may as well go for the lion's lair. If American foreign policy was to be her game, then the only genuinely ethical course seemed to be to avoid the pretense of a morally neutral job at the State Department, where she could fool herself into thinking that her work was clean, that it was the bad guys across the Potomac who were engaged in dirty tricks. *Wenn schon, denn schon*, as the Viennese said. If you're going to do it, you may as well go all the way. The interviews had been intrusive, the background checks had been even worse, and, at the end of the day, when the Agency had informed her that she had not been accepted for employment, while the State Department had told her that she had passed the foreign service exam, the humiliation was complete. But she took the Foggy Bottom job anyway. After all, half a loaf was better than none. Then came the training, the foreign languages, the research jobs, the initial posting abroad. And then, horror of horrors, the Wall came down in Berlin, and communism was over and the Soviet Union was dead and we had won the cold war and history had ended. She had spent several years in Berlin, tracking East Germany's disappearance, and Nigeria, visiting off-shore oil rigs. Then a few years in Bucharest, at precisely the time that the country seemed to be sinking to unimaginable depths of poverty and despair. And then, two years ago, they transferred her to the *Insel der Seligen*, and her initial reaction to the island of the blessed that was Austria was to breathe a sigh of relief. After close to a decade of watching societies undergo death agonies in the forlorn hope that their torments would give birth to a better life, it was a relief to find yourself in a predictable environment of petty politics, coffee, cake, and high-calorie *Schlag*. Very soon, however, the relief had turned to boredom and then to annoyance and resentment. Investigating these murders only made things worse, reminding her of what she had always suspected—that her hopes of seeing action were as absurd as her entry into the CIA had been doomed.

It was time to go. Jane crumpled the wrapper and dropped it into a small receptacle attached to a lamppost on the way down the stairs.

All organizations in Austria had to register with the Ministry of Internal Affairs—that was the law—and Jane knew she'd be able to discover more about the Mir Foundation there. Her contact at the ministry was a portly Austrian from Graz, Harald Schliefsteiner, a perpetually tired-looking *Beamter* who sported short-sleeve shirts and a bow tie at all times of the year. Jane liked him, and he liked her, as evidenced by his tendency to lapse into his native Styrian dialect after several minutes of conversation. At that point, although grateful for the intimacy, Jane had to strain all her German-language skills to make her way through the linguistic maze that his talking became.

Schliefsteiner kissed her on both cheeks.

"*Wie geht's, liebe* Jane?" he said. "How are you?" He took her coat and directed her to a finely upholstered chair.

"That is quite an election campaign," he said. "You must be very excited."

"Not really, Harald," she smiled. "It's one of the benefits of the Foreign Service that you don't have to follow American politics."

"I meant in Ukraine. The opposition appears to be quite strong."

"Oh, yes. Of course. I suppose it is."

"We have," he continued, "reports that *die Russen* are doing everything to keep the 'party of power' in power."

"Yes. I've seen similar reports." Jane looked at her watch. "Well, it's their country. The Ukrainians, I mean."

"Their country, their troubles, right?" said Schliefsteiner. "But that's not why you are here, is it? To talk about the old country."

Schliefsteiner opened a small file and carefully spread its contents on his desk. "*Ja, meine liebe Jane, hier ist es.*"

Yes, here it was, the whole packet of registration materials, including exact details about the financing, organizational structure, mission, and staffing. Pyotr Mironov, the Russian oil and gas magnate, had established the foundation in the mid-nineties, claiming that he wanted to "return to society what society had given him." Yeah right, thought Jane, more like what he had taken from society. The foundation had an endowment of one billion dollars deposited in an Austrian bank. Virsky and his secretary seemed to be the only people working for the organization in Vienna; other offices were located in Berlin, Istanbul, Cyprus, and Tel Aviv. A staff of only four serviced the head office, in Moscow. That was odd. Shouldn't it be the other way around? After all, if you really want to help the Russians, why not disburse the money in Russia to Russians and retain only a small representative office abroad? Mironov was too rich and too smart not to have known that. And too well connected. His biographical details, although presented in sanitized form, showed as much. He had worked as first secretary of one of the Moscow districts of the Communist Party. He had been, secretly, a reformer, yearning for an end to the injustice perpetuated by Leonid Brezhnev and his cronies. His chance came with Mikhail Gorbachev's elevation to head of the Party. Mironov supported glasnost and perestroika enthusiastically—his biography even hinted at his possible authorship of both concepts—Mironov cared only about the good of the people, Mironov wanted democracy, Mironov wanted peace, Mironov wanted prosperity. But then everything fell apart, and somehow poor Mironov, the frustrated democrat, became a billionaire. But a billionaire with a heart.

Jane knew this story all too well. What the biography didn't say she could guess. Mironov parlayed his Communist Party connections into insider information that, during the Wild West days of early capitalism in Russia, meant acquiring enormous mining assets at bargain basement prices. Mironov the democrat, Mironov the humanist lover of mankind, was a corrupt son of a bitch, a robber baron, a thief, perhaps even an Al Capone. You didn't become one of the richest men in Russia without getting your hands dirty. And bloody.

"What do you know of the Mir Foundation?" she asked Schliefsteiner, who had unpacked a piece of apple strudel as she was reading the file. He placed it carefully on a porcelain plate, removed a silver fork from his top drawer, and after wiping it on his neatly pressed white handkerchief, deposited a forkful into his mouth.

"Well," Schliefsteiner mumbled between chews, "they are in every respect a perfect citizen." He swallowed and balanced another piece on the fork. As he raised it to his mouth, a slice of apple dropped lazily onto the plate.

"Any ideas about what they're up to? I mean, what they're *really* up to?"

"What does the file say, *meine liebe* Jane? Mir is a 'philanthropic society.' Officially, that's what they're up to."

"And unofficially?"

"Well, that could be anything, *nicht wahr?*"

"Come on, Harald. Any guesses?"

"Unofficially, we suspect that Mironov may be using the foundation for money transfers to the West."

"Money laundering?"

"You'd have to ask him about that. I had in mind something less dramatic—capital flight."

"Is that illegal?"

"There, who knows? Who knows what's legal in Russia? Not even the Russians know that. Here, it's just a bank deposit, foreign direct investment, FDI—call it what you will. Perfectly legal."

"And Austria is more than happy to take it—whatever its origins."

"Of course. But come now, *liebe* Jane. Which country refuses infusions of capital? Certainly not we. And certainly not you. And which country punishes its rich for being rich? Even the Soviet Union didn't do that. So why should great Russia? Why should tiny Austria?"

"You're completely immoral, Harald. You'd even take money from the devil."

"Amoral, *meine liebe* Jane." He raised a piece of strudel to his lips and smiled back. "And only if there were no strings attached."

It was just past four and that day's conference proceedings wouldn't be over for another hour. With time to spare, Jane decided to visit the Heiligenkreuzer-hof, a serene courtyard of ochres, whites, and greens beyond the reach of the tourists, the horse-drawn carriages, and the tour buses. The Hof belonged to a different era, one long past. She strolled along the cobblestones, pausing to take in the church steeple set against the residence walls and the bright blue of the sky. The iron gate at the far end led into Schönlaterngasse, a crooked little street, supposedly Vienna's oldest, that merged with Postgasse at the point where the Ukrainian church, ensconced in the complex of buildings that housed the post office, still stood. She recalled the first time she had attended a service there—the multilayered singing of the beautiful choir, the smell of the incense that filled the church and seeped into the street outside, the bronze plaques commemorating heroic events and individuals unknown to her. The Ukrainian community she had fled from on Long Island, virtually indistinguishable from other Americans both in speech and buying habits, was nothing like this.

It was during her CIA screening that she had learned of a branch of the family in Vienna. The brother of one of her grandfathers or great grandfathers had enrolled in the University of Vienna at the turn of the century. The son of a Greek Catholic priest, he had studied law, married into the family of a Viennese official, and, having survived the Italian front during World War I—he was supposed to have been in several of the Isonzo campaigns—established a successful practice in the first district. He managed to outlast the Depression and, after Austria's annexation by Germany in 1938, became an *Ahnenforscher* investigating the Aryan roots of whoever cared, or needed, to know. He hadn't joined up with the Nazis, but the work he did had disturbed Jane. Not quite a collaborator, but a collaborator of collaborators. At the same time, he provided the Ukrainian nationalist underground with false documents, which eventually got him arrested, incarcerated in the Gestapo prison overlooking the canal, and shot. Did his death atone for his ethical lapses? Oh God, and who am I to sit in judgment on him? His wife had died sometime in the fifties, and their three children were apparently still alive in Vienna. She would have to look them up some day.

Jane entered the church and sat down in one of the foldout chairs arranged before the iconostasis. This, too, was different. The Orthodox and Greek Catholics hid the altar behind a wall of icons, while the Roman Catholics brazenly displayed what was in reality just a big dining room table. Stern-looking Fathers of the Church, scepters in their hands, glared at her. The Madonna, child cradled in her arms, had an inexplicably sad appearance. Christ the Pantocrator, surrounded by light-headed angels, stared down from the ceiling. Their church in Long Island had been like the malls that surrounded it—sterile, clean, wooden, and white. Luck of the draw that I should have been condemned to a childhood in that dreadful place.

Her parents had come to the United States as refugees after the war. Long Island, with its boring sameness, seemed like paradise after the ruin and devastation of Europe. They had come with her grandmother, baba, whom she remembered as perpetually sitting on a lawn chair in the backyard, kerchief tied about her head even in the summertime, her cane at her feet, reading a newspaper with incomprehensible letters. Her parents and baba spoke only of back home, continuing to live in a world that no longer existed, referring to her neighbors the Antonellis, McSherrys, and Selnicks as the "foreigners." What Jane knew of back home she had learned from their incessant reminiscences—especially baba's—from her interminable accounts of her youth, her loves, the war, the *Bolsheviki.* Baba spoke to her in Ukrainian, and Jane understood every word, every slurring, every cluck, even though her own ability to speak the language was limited. It didn't matter. Baba didn't need a conversationalist, but a listener. And Jane listened, not because she wanted to, but because there was no escaping the constant drone of baba's memories.

Baba's husband had joined the millions of Europeans who flooded America's shores in the early part of the twentieth century. Like so many other Slavs, he first found work in the Pennsylvania coal mines, somewhere near Scranton, but gave that up and moved to New England's boomtown, Fall River, with his Polish friend, Janusz. He stayed there during World War I, but his three brothers were called up for duty in the Austrian military. Within a few months of the outbreak of the war, all three were killed in Bosnia. Jane's mother had photographs of them, dressed in uniforms, sabers at their sides, their neatly combed mustaches pointing upward. There was also an old brown-and-white photograph of her grandfather, stiff white collar, tie, work apron, and flowing mustache, standing in his workshop, shoes and leather remnants and instruments strewn about on the worktable.

Baba took the boat to America right after the war. They bought a small house at the bottom of one of Fall River's famously steep hills, in the Portuguese neighborhood, and he opened a shoe-repair shop. On the way to school, baba said, your mother would buy a doughnut at the corner bakery. Her dark eyes, black hair, and olive complexion resembled those of our neighbors. Is this really your child? the Portuguese would joke. The beach was several hundred feet away. Stefan, Slava, and your mother would go there with pails and collect snails. They would leave their shoes at home and go barefoot. I would cook the snails in a large pot and they would pick them out with hairpins. Stefan liked pulling them out, but hated the sight and smell of them. You know what your mother liked best, Ivanka? The ragman, sitting on his lazy wagon, holding a whip, collecting rags. And the sound of the bell, and the old nag, clip-clopping, clip-clopping, blinkers on its eyes, its tail swaying. The ragman always wore a cap that covered his eyes. And you know what frightened your mother most, Ivanka? The Gypsies who lived next door. They would sit on the stoop, the fat old woman and her five children. Her large colored skirt draped over her fat thighs, her dirty feet in old sandals, a green scarf wrapped around her head, strands of black hair falling into her dark face, a cigarette in her hand. The dark children in their dirty shirts and dirty shorts, scurrying about like mice. Her glare, their laughter.

Three children were born before her grandfather died in 1925, at the age of thirty-five. They buried him without a headstone in some anonymous burial grounds. Baba sold the house and shop and took the children back home. There she married a widower with two children and bore two more. The twenties and thirties were bad times in Poland. They lived in a brick house, on ulica Warszawska, but with seven children, and the Depression, could barely make ends meet. Mama's brother, Stefan, returned to America in the mid-thirties.

Mama was going to join him in 1939. She had an American passport, and she even bought tickets for the boat. Her departure was scheduled for October, but after Molotov and Ribbentrop signed their secret pact and Poland was divided between Nazi Germany and the Soviet Union in September, leaving Stalin's half became impossible. So she stayed. The mass arrests followed soon thereafter, and when the Germans invaded in June 1941, they were greeted as liberators. It was then that the retreating Soviets tortured and killed Slava's husband, a nationalist since the late twenties, along with dozens of other boys. His eyes were gouged out, and his severed tongue and penis were stuffed into his mouth. Only one boy survived the massacre by hiding in the wheat fields; he reappeared the next day, his formerly dark hair a blazing white.

It was toward the end of the forties that Jane's mother and aunt returned to the United States. Stefan had changed since leaving home. He had served in the army and then settled down in New York's Lower East Side. Soon after mama and Slava moved in with him they noticed that Stefan was taking leave of his mind. He said the police were after him, that the Queen of England was persecuting him. Once, he cut the veins in his calves. My blood has been poisoned, he cried. Her mother called the doctor, who had Stefan committed to a hospital on Long Island, where he lived out the rest of his miserable life. Jane never met him. Were it not for the fact that one day he escaped and rang their doorbell, she would never have known he existed. The hospital called, telling mama that her brother had disappeared, and would we know where he is? Jane always wondered how he got out. Did he just walk through the front door? Or did he have to sneak out, perhaps plan his escape for weeks, even months? And how did he get to their home? Did he have money for the bus? Mama said he was short-tempered when she visited him and smoked incessantly, but that he was always glad when she brought cheese and kasha dumplings with sautéed onions and sour cream.

It must've been around here, Jane suddenly realized, that her father had fled from a Soviet patrol looking to repatriate Soviet citizens. *So you must have been in this church, just like I am now.* The jeep shot out from behind the post office as I was walking along the Postgasse. I ran down the street, past the Domini-kanerkirche, and turned left. I dashed through an open door, down two flights, my hat in my hand, my long coat flapping about my terrified knees. And there, in a huge vaulted underground room was a smoke-filled *Keller*, packed with Viennese, sitting at long wooden tables, chatting, drinking wine, eating. I stumbled inside, the waiters looked at my disheveled appearance and motioned me to a table. Wine? they asked. *Ja, ja,* is all I could say. Good God, I am back in my bunker, is all I could think.

Tato had been born and raised in a tiny village set on a hill just above a river bend. A church and bell tower hailed from the seventeenth century, a strange mound may have been the site of a fortress, a crooked cemetery lay at the end of one of the dirt roads. A photograph of her father as a five-year old shows him wearing a white dress and holding a straw hat, his face set in a determined scowl, while standing on a stool next to his mother. Her long, sad face is enveloped in a black kerchief. Another photograph, from the thirties, shows tato standing with some busty girls near a fence. They are smiling and he is grinning, his cap slanted, his eyes drunk. Weddings, he would say, especially those that lasted three days, were a good time to get drunk and take part in brawls. The men would polish their shoes with spit, the women would wear their best blouses. The band played fiddles, drums, and cymbals. We stood in the back of the hall, leaning against the wall, cigarettes in our mouths.

The Soviet occupation of Poland opened the door to university studies. But then came the war, induction into the Red Army, and desertion. In September, together with a group of friends, he surrendered to the Germans and was interned in a POW camp near Dnipropetrovsk. The soup was miserable, the soldiers slept huddled on the ground in a drafty barracks, and the guards beat them with whips. They were released in November, and he walked home. Seven years in the nationalist underground followed—organizing networks, writing propaganda, distributing leaflets, collecting weapons, shooting Germans, planting explosives, killing Soviets. He didn't talk much about those years. It was a bad time, tato would say. Terrible things happened. She never asked: Did you do terrible things? Did terrible things happen to you?

In 1948, after the underground had been smashed, he crossed the border to Czechoslovakia and fled, via Prague and Vienna, to Germany. Munich was in ruins, but it was safe in the American zone, far from the Soviets and their spies and kidnappers. The city was a haven for east European refugees, nationalists and non-nationalists alike. Vicious struggles were transplanted to German soil. Battles were fought for the hearts and minds of the displaced persons, the DP camps became fortresses of political influence, and the ruins were convenient places to dump the bodies of enemies and traitors. But most of all, Munich was heaven for the thousands of Ukrainians assembled in the camps. They were young, energetic, passionate, and strong. They had nothing to do but recreate their homelands, to flirt, to date, to drink and play cards, to forget the war, to prepare for the next war, to dream about what they had and about what they might have. He lived in a camp for one year and then got his own room in a badly damaged building across the Isar.

Window washing was all he was good for in America. The trick to washing a window well was, he used to tell Jane, in the water. *Yes, tell me about the squeegee, tell me only about the squeegee.* You always had to wipe enough onto the window. And you had to repeat the process. If there wasn't enough water, the squeegee would drag across the pane, squeak, leave streak marks. It could even break the window. The other trick was in the movement of the squeegee. You had to start at the top and then, with quick horizontal strokes, work your way downward, always making sure that they overlapped just a bit. But that could be tricky—*oh yes, very tricky, but I think I've got it*—because if you overlapped too much, then the squeegee was likely to move across a dry pane and break it. If you worked quickly, you could wash the whole window in less than a minute. That was the trick, Ivanka, see? *You know what, tato? I'm going to wash windows when I grow up.*

Jane crossed herself—something she hadn't done in years—stood up and walked out of the church. She turned right on Postgasse, and, after a left on Rotenturmstrasse, returned to St. Stephen's Square within a few minutes. She took Kärntnerstrasse—a name that struck her as being completely unpronounceable the first time she had encountered it—did some window-shopping at the lingerie stores and, just before the Opera, turned right to reach the Sacher. Professor Bird was standing in front of the hotel, smoking.

"Here again?" he said frostily. "The spook business must be slow."

"How's your hand?" Jane snapped.

Bird turned a bright red, flicked the cigarette into the street—only an American would do that, she thought—and pushed the door. Jane followed him into the lobby and saw him join two other men. She approached the group with outstretched hand.

"Professor Bird!" she cried. "What a pleasure and what a surprise!"

Bird turned red again, coughing and fingering his tie as he extended his hand. Jane noticed that he still wore his high school ring.

"Mizz Sweet," he said. "An unexpected pleasure. This is Mizz Jane Sweet, who says she's the cultural attaché at the U.S. Embassy. But that's not all Mizz Sweet is, gentlemen. Mizz Sweet is also proof of our government's enlightened policies of multiculturalism. She is a hyphenated American. May I call you that, Mizz Sweet? A Ukrainian-American, right? And that hyphen, my dear friends"—he turned to his colleagues—"means that she hasn't a trace of anti-Semitism in her.

"May I introduce you to my colleagues, Mizz Sweet? Professor Albert Foxx of New York University and Professor Heinrich Zeppelin of Vienna University."

"Delighted, Miss Sweet. That's Foxx with two x's."

"*Enchanté, gnädige Frau.*" Zeppelin bowed.

"Professor Foxx," continued Bird with a broad grin, "is a world-renowned specialist in Jewish history. Professor Zeppelin is the author of the famous *Transformationstheorie.* I sit at the fount of their wisdom."

"*Ach, nein,*" countered Zeppelin. "It is I who learns from you. Did you know, Madame, that Professor Bird has just received the Oblomov Prize? It is a great honor, a tremendous honor." Zeppelin paused. "It is, *lieber Kollege,* the Transformations*kritik*theorie. But no matter."

Jane was at a loss for words. Bird's insinuation, that all Ukrainians were congenital anti-Semites, did not upset her. She had long since gotten used to that kind of casual xenophobia in the diplomatic corps and had learned to ignore it. What did shock her was his brazenness. The racists she knew usually spoke behind her back.

"What—" Jane asked, "what is the prize for?"

"My dear Miss Sweet," said Foxx, "the Oblomov Prize is the greatest honor that the profession can bestow on its practitioners. It—"

"—is nothing," said Bird. "I hardly—"

"Tell me," Jane broke in, "have any of you seen Professor Bazarov?"

"Bazar-roff?" asked Zeppelin. "Who is Bazar-roff?"

"Oh, you know," replied Bird. "Igor Bazarov. The sociologist from Columbia. No one's seen him in a few days. That right, Mizz Sweet?"

"Did he write that book on subjectivity?" asked Zeppelin.

"Yes," replied Bird, "something about the ontology of subjectivity. Or is it epistemology? Pretty dreadful stuff."

"Only *entsetzlich*?" Zeppelin took a deep breath. "It was *ein Skandal!* He plagiarized, you know. The work of Babitskaya. She is furious. She will never forgive him. And you know what that means."

"Will Tanya sue?" asked Foxx. "It's those damned Russians. They all do it. They think they're still"—he pointed in some undefined direction with his thumb—"there."

"*Nein*," said Zeppelin. "She is preparing something much much better—a massive article, an expose, for *Transgressions Review*. I have seen the first draft. It is devastating. It will kill that Bazar-roff."

Jane noticed Virsky enter the lobby, the statuesque and scantily clad Masha on his arm. Heads turned, and there was an audible drop in the sound level of the conversations. The male professors were visibly leering; the females adopted poses of refined disgust. Jane was beginning to like Virsky. Anyone with such chutzpah couldn't be all bad—even if he was an evasive slime. No less important, his appearance gave her the perfect excuse to escape.

"Excuse me, gentlemen," she said. "This has been most enlightening."

"Please do come again," said Bird. "Any time." Foxx and Zeppelin bowed.

As Jane walked away, she caught Virsky's eye.

"Excellent Madame Sweet!" he cried, visibly delighted. "You meet my secretary, have you?"

"Herr Virsky, what a pleasure. You wouldn't know where Professor Bazarov is, would you?"

"Igor Alexandrovich is vigorous man, Madame Sweet. If he is not at conference, I am being sure he is somewhere else. Yes, Mashenka?"

"He is *khuy*," she hissed.

"You see, Madame. Mashenka is not liking our friend Bazarov. But at one time she is." He turned to Masha. "No? Most women are."

"Most men are," she glared.

"So you think he's shacked up somewhere with some woman?" asked Jane.

"Let us just be saying that probably Professor Bazarov is doing field work," answered Virsky, "and that he is having his hands no doubt quite full."

"Jane!" Bristol caught up with her on the stairs. "Your friend at the interior ministry called. Left a message about someone named Zabarov."

"And?"

"Said he did some checking. Apparently this Zabarov character boarded an Austrian Airlines flight to Kiev two days ago. Here's his number, if you want to call back."

Jane took the slip of paper. "Thanks, Bristol. I may owe you lunch for that."

Jane walked past the secretaries with deliberate slowness, glancing at each one's desk but saying nothing. As she instinctively raised her hand, she decided not to knock. The ambassador was standing at the window as she walked in.

"Did you ever wonder how this city manages to survive, Sweet? Look, they're tearing up the road again. Now why the hell are they doing that? They fixed the road and the tram tracks last year, and the year before that, and the year before that." He pulled back the curtain.

"I have a progress report on those three academics, sir."

The ambassador said nothing.

"I'm not exactly sure what they were up to, but they received some big money from a shady Russian foundation and—"

"And what?"

"There's a fourth academic, sir, and he's in Kiev. That's in—"

"I know where it is, Sweet."

"I don't know why he's there, sir, but I think I should talk to him."

"You're Russian," said the ambassador. "Go to fucking Russia and talk to him."

C H A P T E R 5

▼

Breathing heavily, *too* heavily, Anatoly Sergeevich Filatov climbed the stairs to Titov's apartment. The lightbulbs were missing, and the staircase was almost pitch black. His shoes scraped against the raw concrete steps. His right hand held the sticky banister, his left was in his pocket. The stench emanating from the garbage chute was overpowering. Why do all Soviet buildings stink alike? Is there nothing else in this country except for cabbage, cooking oil, and urine? Some animal scurried past him, brushing against his leg. A man's voice, agitated and angry, exploded in bursts. The nervous twangs of a guitar floated down from an upper floor.

He carefully opened the three deadbolt locks on the door. To the left was the kitchen, straight ahead was the bedroom, to the right was the living room where Bazarov slept. He waited for his eyes to adjust to the darkness and turned the locks shut. As he made his way gingerly forward, he stumbled on a shoe. A few more steps with his arms outstretched and he entered the living room and sat down on the sofa. The position was perfect. The table—along with the samovar that stood atop it—would hide him. The doorway, softly illuminated by the grayness filtering in through the kitchen window, provided a perfect outline for anyone stepping inside. Filatov loosened his tie, checked the gun, made sure that the silencer was screwed on properly, and removed a book from his inside jacket pocket. Bazarov was out, probably whoring around. He had time.

Filatov laughed silently as he pictured himself. Here I am, sitting in a darkened room in a filthy Soviet house, waiting for some insignificant man to appear in that doorway so that I can kill him. I am surrounded by Soviet smells, and although I cannot see the colors and fabrics and furniture in this room, I know exactly how it looks. I have been in such rooms thousands of times. I spent all my life fighting for the right of people to live in just these kinds of rooms, and now that the fight is over, I am confined to one myself. I live the life of rag pickers and derelicts rummaging about trash heaps and rubble. Is this what they mean by poetic justice?

Unfortunately, the trash that really mattered had begun to pile up long before. He had joined the secret police because he sincerely believed that the enemies of socialism had to be stopped, that socialism was, with all its flaws, worth defending, that the alternative, capitalism, was infinitely worse. It was in the late sixties that things had begun to change. The Communist Party—the party of the great Lenin! the vanguard of the working class! the wise parent of the world's proletarian masses!—had become a collection of clerks, of pencil pushers, of bureaucrats, of fat little men with fat little ambitions. The KGB, which consisted of the best and the brightest, the true believers, the priests, managed to retain its elan for a few more years. But, by the seventies, even most of his comrades in the secret police cared more about East German washing machines and American jeans than about communism. Service in the KGB then became a daily test of faith. If you really believed, if you believed to the point of not countenancing any doubts whatsoever, you could survive, you could do your job, you could see the larger picture. But as soon as a tiny doubt crept in—Was Leonid Brezhnev really a genius? Were we really catching up with the West? Did the non-Russian nationalities really love their Russian brothers?—it became impossible to remain an unwavering member of the priesthood.

He had no qualms about his specialty—"wet work." Assassinations had a religious quality to them. It was almost as if their wetness was a form of baptism. Priests baptized you as a sign of your joining the church. He baptized his victims as a sign of their leaving the church. Did they all deserve to die? Yes, they did, and he knew that. Filatov always checked their backgrounds meticulously. He never just carried out orders blindly. Although he had sworn obedience to the order of the KGB, he knew that it was his duty to be certain that all who died by his hand deserved to die by his hand. Looking back, Filatov realized that this was his undoing. The more committed he had become to being a conscientious assassin—and that word, conscientious, was just right, because he always squared each assassination with the moral demands of his conscience—the more he realized that his superiors were ethically indifferent. They had not only abandoned the priesthood: they were heretics. When you are the only believer in a church of unbelievers, what then?

Filatov took the book in his hands and raised it to his nose. It smelled good. The Cyrillic characters were reassuring. He had found it in Moscow, in a used bookstore on the Arbat. The author—an Englishman—was unknown to him, but the title had immediately appealed to him: there was a time, once, when *we* had the power and *we* exalted in the glory. He had finished the book in one sitting. He recalled, still, how it had captivated him. *Whiskey priest*: the phrase resonated. It stuck in his mind. It was a few days later that, in what could only be called an epiphany, he had realized why. He had been crossing Red Square, when he suddenly noticed what should have been obvious to him long before—that the formerly long lines of pilgrims before the Lenin Mausoleum had disappeared. The churchgoers had vanished and the church had fallen into desuetude and he had become a whiskey priest. He had begun to doubt his calling, his very faith—in the KGB and, worst of all, in communism—long before. But that day on Red Square—the massive walls of the Kremlin laid out before him like an unbreachable barrier—he knew that he was alone. Could you still be a priest if God refused to answer your prayers? If God ignored you? If God turned away from you? He continued to perform his duties, but he did so perfunctorily, without conviction, without passion. When he killed now, he merely killed. He no longer baptized. Why kill? Why not kill? It made no difference.

But oh what a difference it had at one time made! In imperialist Germany, its revanchist claws set to pounce on the German Democratic Republic, wet work had been both inspiring and inspirational. It had required every ounce of his passion and courage; it was a real test of faith. As religious ritual the kidnapping of Hans Jürgen Vogel had, he recalled, been flawless. They had played their parts perfectly—the priests, the altar boys, the chorus. He remembered how the heavy black car turned into the leafy street, its driver releasing the steering wheel and accelerating as the turn was completed. The important man in the back seat probably stretched his legs and looked out the darkened windows. At that moment our cars rammed the Mercedes from behind and blocked him in front. The driver turned the wheel, to the left, to the right, accelerating, going into reverse. By then Vogel must have known what awaited him. We jumped out, spraying the Mercedes with gunfire, puncturing its tires, blasting its motor, shattering its windshield. The driver jerked backwards and forwards and then to the side and then he fell over, embracing the wheel with his limp body, his arms at his side, his cap on the floor. We yanked open the back door and grabbed Vogel's arms and legs and, as his shoe fell off and his briefcase opened, sending a cavalcade of papers to the ground, we dragged him across the glass-strewn asphalt, lifted him like a sacrificial lamb and dropped him, hands and feet tied, mouth stuffed with rags and newspaper, into the pit of the trunk. The wheels screeched as we pulled away from the smoking wreck. We raced down the Autobahn, along the country roads, our lips pressed together, sweat pouring down our foreheads, our eyes glistening. When we reached the house and opened the trunk, Vogel lay whimpering, the newspaper moist with saliva, his crotch wet, an overpowering stench emanating from the pit. The heroism of exploiters, we laughed. We spat at him, dragged him into the cellar, and threw him onto the black floor. Now you will see how the people live, we said.

The police were everywhere, their guns poised, their dogs sniffing nervously; the portly women in their little green hats eyed everyone suspiciously; neighbors looked through their peepholes, watching who came, who went. We hid in barren apartments, smoking, sleeping on stained mattresses, making love with lips pressed tight, teeth biting tongues, eating noodles and rice and noodles and rice, sifting through the garbage, careful not to flush the toilet too often or too infrequently, walking barefoot on the cold floor, drinking too much beer and wine to make the time pass. But those inconveniences amounted to nothing as soon as we began planning an *Aktion*. That was when the pulse quickened and we forgot everything, where we were and how we slept and what we ate. Whom do you kill if the entire capitalist class is guilty? Why him and why not her? The bourgeois press called us terrorists, but ours was really the deepest sense of morality. We did not just kill so as to kill. We killed for a purpose. They killed for no reason at all, dropping bombs on peasants, dropping bombs on children. They were the terrorists. And when we finally agreed on whom to eliminate, there was the vitally important question of how. How do you ambush an imperialist's car if you are constantly being watched and he is constantly being guarded? Figuring that out, pulling it off, pressing the trigger or the button, listening to the explosion, running, running, opening the door, pressing the trigger, dragging, pulling, pushing, shouting—*that* was what made you alive. An *Aktion* breathed life into you. During an *Aktion* you forgot who you were and where you were. After, as your blood raced through your body, as your mind exploded and your heart leapt, you knew exactly who you were. You knew exactly why you were alive. Your life had meaning, because life had meaning.

That was then. And now? Filatov looked at his watch. It was close to eleven, and Bazarov would probably be returning home soon. He checked the silencer again and placed the gun on a cushion next to him. With any luck he would be in bed before midnight. A large drink, perhaps in the hotel bar, would be good—no, imperative.

Igor Alexandrovich Bazarov slept late that day, and when he got up just before noon both Titov and Vika were already gone. Too bad. He was in the mood for Vika. He shaved, drank some of the tea that she had prepared, and after putting on his shirt and suit—the good Vika, he noticed, had cleaned and ironed all his clothes—went outdoors. The cloudless sky illuminated the pale blue buildings of the Podol. The crumbling sidewalks were shrouded in shade. A red-haired dog lay sprawled near an overflowing garbage receptacle. He walked to a nearby cafe—the hand-painted sign said, simply, Kafe—and sat down at a corner table, the wall at his back, the door at his front. A tall thin waitress, her lips red and her dark hair pulled back in a bun, glanced at him indifferently. He ordered an espresso and a cognac and lit a cigarette.

He was safe now, but he had to assume that the assassin would soon find his tracks. He had been twenty minutes ahead of him in Vienna; he might be anywhere from several hours to several days ahead of him now. But this was no time to be complacent. These people were professionals. He knew that. And he was not. He knew that too. His only advantage lay in the killer's not fully knowing where he was and what he planned to do. That was a small advantage, but so far it had meant the difference between life and death.

He couldn't stay in Kiev indefinitely. Too many people knew him. Sooner or later someone would see him and word would get out. Vilen Vladimirovich could probably be trusted, at least for a few days. That meant he'd have to move on. But where? And where was he ultimately to go? Fleeing endlessly was not an attractive prospect. His money would run out, his wits would run out, and besides, who wanted to run with no prospect of rest? For the time being, his priority had to be to stay one step ahead of the killer. But he also needed to eliminate the threat for good. That meant either capturing or killing the killer. He couldn't do that on his own, and although the local boys in Kiev or Moscow were efficient, they couldn't be trusted with such a job. Besides, he didn't have the time.

It was obvious. It was so obvious that Bazarov had to smile. Running from Vienna had been a natural, and perfectly understandable, impulse. But it had been, on second thought, a grievous mistake. Here, he was vulnerable. Although he knew the people and the places, the killer surely knew them better—or knew people who knew them better. In the West, on the other hand, he was on familiar terrain. There, he was a respected professor, and an American citizen to boot. Here, he was an émigré. There, the killer would be the stranger. There, the advantage would be with him, not the killer. It was obvious. He had to get back to Vienna. He would go to the Austrian police or to Interpol or to the American embassy. The persecuted professor. The prisoner of conscience. The dissident. The Salman Rushdie of the post-Soviet world. I can go into hiding, if necessary. I can write op-ed pieces for major newspapers. Amnesty International will defend me.

Bazarov finished the cognac and ordered another hundred grams. The airport would be dangerous. They'd be watching it. He would take the train. He'd go to Lvov and then take a plane or a train back to Vienna. But he wouldn't take the overnighter to Lvov. They might be expecting him to try that. No, he'd take the *elektrichka*, the commuter train. It would take longer, but it'd be safer. Most of the passengers would be workers and peasants, and it would be relatively easy to spot someone who could walk the streets of Vienna unnoticed. He'd leave tomorrow morning. As for today, why not relax a bit and have some fun? He had time. No reason to kill yourself.

Bazarov motioned to the waitress and she brought him the bill. He left some money on the table, smiled at her on his way out, and decided to take a stroll along the Dniepr. The streets were quiet. No one seemed to be following him. In a few minutes he reached the promenade and turned right. The harbor to his left was silent, and except for an occasional motorboat, the river was empty, its waters reflecting the bright orange sun. He continued past the river port, where two cruise boats lay in berth, and soon reached the pedestrian bridge that led to the island. He stopped at a small restaurant for a beer, and then went to the beach, where, after wrapping himself tightly in his coat, he lay down on the grass and fell asleep. His last conscious thought was of his student days in Kiev, when weekend outings to this very spot had been *de rigeur*. Wasn't it here that he had lost his virginity?

Who had it been—Alyona or Alyosha? He had been to this place with both of them on many occasions. Alyona usually set out the salads and cut the bread, while he and Alyosha had grilled the shashlik. They drank wine and vodka and, on national holidays, even champagne. And then, sated, they lay on the blanket, their straw hats pulled over their eyes, asleep. Who was it that awoke him? Alyona or Alyosha? Who was it that undid his zipper while he slept and mounted him? Alyona or Alyosha? Bazarov could not remember. No matter: eventually he would be sleeping with both.

The sun was in the west when he awoke. The beach was empty, and he felt cold. Bazarov brushed the fine sand from his pants and coat and slowly walked back to the city. It was dark when he entered the bar at the foot of Andrew's Ascent, a cobblestone street that wound its way from the Podol to St. Andrew's

Cathedral at the top of one of Kiev's many hills. The music was loud and Bazarov could barely make out the darkened faces that turned his way. He sat at the bar and ordered a cognac. The young man sitting beside him asked him for a cigarette. As Bazarov opened his cigarette case, the young man's gaze lingered on his face. Bazarov returned the stare and offered to light the cigarette.

"My name is Kolya," said the young man.

"Igor," replied Bazarov.

"Delighted to make your acquaintance, Igorchik."

"The pleasure is all mine, Kolya."

Several hours later the two men straggled out of the bar.

"It is not far from here, *malchik*," said Bazarov. "Be patient, little one, we have all night."

They walked silently. Drunks passed them; twice they encountered couples feverishly groping at clothes and body parts in the shadows. Cars occasionally rattled along the uneven streets. Bazarov listened. But besides Kolya's excited breathing he could hear nothing—no footsteps, no sounds.

"Here," he whispered to Kolya. "We are here. Follow me, but be very quiet. My friends are home and we will have to be very quiet."

They climbed the stairs, Kolya's hand touching his buttocks, as much for guidance as for pleasure. Bazarov opened the locks, turned the doorknob quietly, and pressed against the door. It emitted a low squeak. He raised the knob and pressed again. This time the door opened silently. He put a finger to his lips and pointed to the entrance to the living room.

"You go ahead," he whispered. "I'll close the door. Be very quiet."

Kolya nodded as he stepped inside the living room.

Bazarov heard a slight whistle, and then he saw Kolya's body fall backwards against the kitchen door.

It was only after he emerged from the house, his breath short and his head bursting, and ran into the shadows across the street that he realized that his killer had found him.

Filatov placed the gun in his holster and calmly rose from the sofa. This had been easier than he had expected. Bazarov's silhouette had been visible against the frame of the doorway and all he had to do was, literally, point and shoot. He turned on the lights and walked over to the body. It was slumped against the wall, head bent forward, a sticky red stain covering the chest. Filatov grabbed the hair and raised the head. Who the hell was *this*?

He returned to the living room and examined Bazarov's briefcase. Some underwear, a shirt, a tie, a pair of socks, but what he was looking for, his passport, wasn't inside. Filatov straightened the sofa cover and turned off the lights. Titov would have something to worry about when he got home, but Titov would know what to do. In the meantime, he would have to resume the hunt. He carefully closed the door and slowly descended the coal-black stairs. As he approached the first landing, it hit him and he had to laugh. So Bazarov also liked boys!

Several blocks away on Doroshenko Street Bazarov came upon a taxi parked in front of a brightly lit grill bar. The driver, black cap, black leather jacket, and crumpled pants, was standing at the window, eating a frankfurter and drinking beer.

"Your car?" Bazarov asked. The man nodded.

"Would you like to make some real money?"

"How much?" the driver asked.

"Two hundred dollars. You drive me to Lvov."

"When?"

"Right away."

"In a hurry, aren't you?" said the driver. "Five hundred."

"Three. Take it or leave it. There are other taxis around."

"Three-fifty."

Bazarov began walking away.

"Very well," cried the driver. "Three."

"One now"—Bazarov opened his wallet—"two when we get there."

"Get in." The man climbed into the front seat and turned on the ignition. "Do you have any cigarettes?"

"No."

The car climbed the winding street that led to the city center. They turned left just before reaching the Khreshchatyk. A few minutes later they were on the road that led west. Endless rows of lonely high-rise buildings stretched out on both sides. Until, suddenly, they stopped and a forest appeared. Bazarov looked through the rear window and watched the lights of the city recede and, finally, disappear.

Filatov walked along the dark streets of the Podol, occasionally breaking the silence by hitting a can with his foot. He stopped at a tree to relieve himself, listening to his urine strike the bark and trickle to the ground. The sound was a comforting counterpoint to the clattering cans. He found a kiosk and ordered a beer.

"Do you have anything stronger?" he asked the man inside.

"Depends."

"On what?"

"On how much money you have."

Filatov slid him a twenty-dollar bill and received a bottle of Ukrainian pepper vodka and two plastic cups in exchange. He filled both and gave one to the man.

"*Za nas*," Filatov said. "To us," the man replied.

Half an hour and some ten cups later, Filatov discarded the bottle in the large trashcan and resumed his walk to the hotel. He used a public phone to call Kostenko who promised to get his boys scouring the streets immediately. Then he called Titov's mobile phone, apologizing for the mess in his hallway. "*Eto nichevo*," said Titov, "it's nothing." That, unfortunately, was true. All his troubles had ended in nothing. One homosexual was dead, and Bazarov was still on the loose. He decided that he would pay Shevchenko another call in the morning.

There was nothing else to be done, for now. Bazarov might be hiding somewhere in Kiev, but that was unlikely. By now he must have realized that Titov had set him up and that the entire Kiev underworld was looking for him. No, Bazarov would try to leave the city. He'd avoid the airport and he'd probably avoid the train station. Which meant that he'd probably try to leave by car. And that meant taking a taxi. He had the money, so he could get the taxi to take him as far as he'd want to go. So where would he go? Where would *I* go, if I were in his shoes? Russia? No, he'd know that if I could find him in Ukraine, I could also find him in Russia. Some godforsaken village? He'd stand out like a sore thumb. It would have to be a city, a big city. Where would you go? Filatov asked himself. I'd try to get out of here, that's what I'd do. I'd go west. It was obvious, he laughed, it was quite obvious. Bazarov would head for Lvov.

The taxi sped past the pine forests west of Kiev. Dilapidated concrete bus stop shelters appeared, like apparitions, and disappeared. An occasional Moskvich passed the taxi on the left. The driver was hunched over the wheel, his black cap slung over his forehead, a cigarette protruding from his mouth. Bazarov sat slumped in the back seat, chain smoking. It would be a long night. He couldn't read—it was too dark for that—he couldn't write, and the thought of spending all these hours with a filthy *taksist* left him feeling nauseous. *Quel horreur.* Why did the great unwashed not wash? Suddenly the car slowed down.

"I have been thinking," the driver said.

"*Da?*" said Bazarov quietly.

"I have been thinking that it must be very important for you to get to Lvov."

"You are very perceptive," replied Bazarov dryly.

"I have also been thinking that such a trip must be worth at least five hundred dollars—three now, two later."

Bazarov reached into his pocket and handed him two hundred-dollar bills.

"Now drive."

The cab driver slowly placed the bills in his pocket. Before accelerating, he took a cigarette from the pack on the dashboard and lit it. After several puffs and a visible grin, he brought the car to 120 kilometers again. This was easy money, and as he thought about the man in the back seat, he decided there was no reason why he should stop at five. The man had the money. In a few hours, just before sunrise, he would try again. And if he refused, he would throw him out.

Bazarov focused his eyes on the back of the driver's head. His unevenly trimmed hair came down over his collar. It was greasy, as if water were a luxury item. The inside of the car stank—from the cheap cigarettes he smoked, from the exhaust, and from the body odor. Welcome to Ukraine. Nothing had changed. These people and everything they touched and did were as filthy as they had always been. The driver coughed and cleared his throat. He opened the window and spat. A drop of phlegm struck Bazarov's cheek. He shuddered, wiping it off with his handkerchief.

Bazarov noticed the trees and the road before him coming into focus. The car had slowed down, its headlights illuminating the empty road and the trees. The driver said nothing as he pulled up onto the shoulder. He put the car into neutral and climbed out. Bazarov watched him take quick short paces and stop at the edge of the forest, where he undid his zipper and leaned back his head. Bazarov quietly opened the back door and slipped into the driver's seat. A few seconds later, as the surprised driver turned his head and let loose a loud curse, Bazarov was already speeding away. Bazarov smiled as he watched him in the rear-view mirror, holding his cock with one hand and waving his cap with the other.

He expected the Khreshchatyk to be empty. Instead, small groups of mostly young people, their faces flush with excitement, stood about. Some were drinking, but most were talking loudly. Filatov slowed his pace. Several boys, all wearing orange scarves, burst into laughter after one of them mentioned the president. A girl was distributing leaflets and pleading, "*golosuyte za Ukrainu.*" How can you vote for Ukraine, Filatov thought, if you don't even speak Ukrainian?

Filatov climbed the steps leading from Independence Square to the Moskva. Short of breath, and feeling unsteady from the pepper vodka, he had to pause mid-way, on the marble platform where Lenin had once stood. The outlines of the pedestal were barely visible. His head spinning, he went into a crouch. Filatov surveyed the square below. The conversations and laughter merged into an insistent buzz. A boy and girl were kissing near the entrance to the post office, his hand on her thigh, her left leg wrapped around his calves. Filatov watched a pair of policemen approach the square from the left. They stopped to look at the couple and then resumed their stroll.

Swaying gently, Filatov climbed the rest of the stairs and—almost expecting it to have vanished—turned again to look at the square. The couple was still there. He took one last breath of fresh air and plunged into the lobby. Except for the late-night clerk reading a book, it was deserted. The door to the bar was open and, after hesitating for a second, Filatov walked in. A party was going on inside. Some woman, obviously the pretext for the event, was speaking loudly, telling jokes, smoking. The men stood around her, listening intently, looking at her breasts. She embraced some man and he patted her head, as if she were his daughter. She whispered in his ear and he laughed, and then she laughed, and then everyone else fell momentarily silent watching them laugh.

"To democracy!" someone cried, "let us drink to democracy." And to peace, someone else said. And to freedom, said a third. They drank. Glasses were quickly refilled and then, after the woman loudly cleared her voice, she suggested that they drink to Ukraine. They drank again. "To truth!" she said, raising her glass high, "because without truth there can be no democracy, no peace, no freedom, and no Ukraine." Everyone cheered her discovery.

Filatov made his way through the crowd to the bar. The blonde, sitting on the same stool, smiled as she saw him. He nodded, and she slid off the stool and followed him into the elevator.

The black Soviet-era telephone rang hesitantly, almost as if it were apologizing for the USSR's collapse. Filatov grabbed the receiver and said *allo*. The voice at the other end was Kostenko's.

"I have some interesting news, Anatoly Sergeevich," it said. "The police have picked up a cab driver, about fifty kilometers west of Kiev, who claims that his taxi was stolen from him last night. I think we may safely conclude that it was our friend."

"What time did this happen?"

"Just a little after midnight."

The blonde was still asleep. Filatov looked at his watch. It was eight. Bazarov would be in Lvov in a few hours.

"You know what to do in Lvov," Filatov said and hung up. The blonde stirred.

"Wake up," he said. "I want you out of here in five minutes."

Upon emerging from the bathroom, Filatov noted with satisfaction that she was gone. He began to dress. His pants lay where he had dropped them last night, crumpled, on the floor, but near them, open, also lay his wallet. The dollars were missing, of course. He had more in his money belt, but that wasn't the issue. I am getting careless, he thought, I am making stupid mistakes—again. What is happening to me?

Filatov had a glass of vodka in the bar, checked out, and climbed into a cab. A light rain was coming down, but the Khreshchatyk was as busy as always. The taxi moved slowly through the traffic. Filatov watched the women wearing high-heeled shoes and sporting excessive amounts of purplish mascara negotiate the puddles. The car turned right at the Univermag department store, its rain-streaked display windows offering blurred glimpses of uninspired arrangements of gadgets and mannequins. The baggy gray suits and beige shoes favored by Soviet bureaucrats were, apparently, still all the rage in Kiev. It would take another five or ten years for the styles currently popular in Moscow to trickle down. Filatov exited the cab near the scaffolding that hid what used to be the Hotel Leipzig in Soviet times. He turned down Vladimirskaya and stepped into the building that housed the Ukrainian security service.

Colonel Shevchenko extended a greasy hand in greeting. His desk, covered with stained newspapers, was littered with the remains of a piece of cured fish.

"Caught it myself," he said half-apologetically. "Near my dacha. Have some." He reached into a drawer and pulled out a bottle. "Just got this yesterday. It was confiscated from a Chechen smuggler." He filled two dirty glasses and handed one to Filatov. They downed the vodka and smacked their lips, almost in unison.

"Have some fish," Shevchenko said. "It's salty." As Filatov took a piece, Shevchenko continued, "And now, my dear friend, how may I help you?"

"You know that Bazarov is on his way to Lvov."

Shevchenko barely nodded.

"And you know that I must find him."

Shevchenko remained still.

"And I must know for certain whether he is still working for you."

"Why?"

"I would not want relations between our two fraternal services to be unintentionally compromised."

"Of course not," Shevchenko replied, "of course not. We are Slavs. We must stick together." He filled both glasses again.

"Exactly."

"Even when we make mistakes."

This time Filatov said nothing.

"He was of no importance to us, Anatoly Sergeevich, but we are a rule of law state. A democracy."

Filatov remained still.

"It was, of course, a robbery," continued Shevchenko. "Kiev has become so unsafe. But we do what we can do. Is that not so, Anatoly Sergeevich? We help our friends, and our friends help us."

"Of course, Taras Grigorovich. I would have it no other way."

"So let us drink to friendship," Shevchenko said, raising his glass.

"To eternal friendship," added Filatov.

One hour later Filatov was sitting in an army plane bound for Lvov. All around him sat sleepy soldiers in olive drab fatigues and maroon berets—commandos of the illustrious Ukrainian armed forces. He looked out the window. The emptiness of this country never failed to amaze him. This wasn't the steppe, which stretched into infinity and produced a sense of claustrophobia in him, but the countryside west of Kiev, with its occasional clumps of forest and houses, still resembled a void. How can people live in the constant presence of nothing?

Filatov tried to make himself comfortable. He closed his eyes and concentrated on the hum of the plane. He had known that Shevchenko would eventually find out about the little man, but for him to have done so in only one day meant either that the Ukrainians had become exceptionally competent overnight or that they had been following him—and that he had not noticed. And that was unforgivable. There was nothing to be done about it. Another lapse, another mistake. It was time to get this over with and go home. He would soon be in Lvov. He would soon finish the job. And then what? And then what, indeed. He would return to Moscow and continue serving his two masters. He recalled having read in the Bible that Christ said that no servant can serve two masters. That if he does, he'll wind up betraying or despising both. The point of the story was that you had to choose. But that was the problem. If forced to choose—and if permitted to choose whatever he wanted—he would opt for neither of his masters. Holy Russia, Mother Russia—she had become a god for many of his comrades, but he could not worship her. At best, Russia would be his stepmother, perhaps an aunt, the kind that always brought you gifts and gave you money. But she'd never be his mother, and she'd never be his God. So who, or what, *was* his God? Communism had died. The Soviet Union had died. Even the KGB was no more. Was anything left? Was there a core, or did you just keep on peeling until, one day, you realized that nothing was left? Had he not realized that already? Was his life not just a habit—something he continued to do only because he had always been doing it and couldn't imagine anything else? But he *could* imagine something else. He could easily imagine nonexistence. The Soviet Union had stopped to exist. Communism no longer existed. Weren't he and his kind next? I have become an existentialist, he thought. I have become an existentialist killer! Filatov laughed, as surprised by this conclusion as by the tears trickling down his face.

Time passed slowly as Bazarov drove toward Lvov. But at least he could think again, and he had much to think about. Back in New York, he would parlay his status as dissident into a demand that the university give him a higher salary or a larger office or a smaller teaching load or more research opportunities or—why settle for small things? Why not go for it all? With a little skill and a little luck he could join the ranks of the superstar professors. And why not? If the others could get away with it—and they claimed to be radicals, Marxists, and leftists concerned only with the good of the oppressed, suppressed, repressed, and depressed—why not he? He might even get the MacArthur Foundation's genius prize. And then he could, like they, devote himself exclusively to battling injustice from his Riverside Drive apartment. But, Bazarov interrupted his own reverie, first things first. First to Lvov, then to Vienna, then to New York. And then we'll see what happens.

At daybreak the flatness of the countryside had disappeared, replaced by the rolling hills of Galicia. He stopped for gas at a spanking new American-style gas station, where a pretty uniformed boy checked his oil and cleaned his windshield. Knots of stumpy men and women stood around the bus shelters, shifting their weight from foot to foot, the men in black hats, the women in brightly colored kerchiefs. Horse-drawn carts, with worn-out automobile tires for wheels, lumbered along the side of the road, their drivers sitting motionlessly with whips in their hands and cigarettes dangling from their lips. The silver domes of churches glistened in the sunlight.

The traffic signs announced that he was in Lvov. The clusters of little houses gave way to Soviet-era high-rises, their facades crumbling, their balconies cluttered with drying laundry, bicycles, tires, empty bottles, and jars of marinated tomatoes. He had been in Lvov once before, in his student days. The city had been a hotbed of nationalism, and Bazarov had spent a semester infiltrating the youth clubs and poetry circles at the university. It had been easy and profitable work. The west Ukrainians were different from the people he knew in Odessa and Kiev, more relaxed as well as more neurotic. They suspected everybody from the east of being a KGB agent, and it hadn't been easy to persuade them that he was on their side. A few well-timed tips saved a few scribblers from arrest, while carefully crafted reports to the KGB enabled the secret police to stumble upon some illicit gatherings. In the end, it wasn't clear to Bazarov that much of anything had been achieved. The nationalists remained active, and the KGB continued to arrest them. The one consolation was that they had placed a few hacks in jail, the ones who thought that goatees and jeans made them daring dissidents and men of the West. But the city had made its impression on him. It was beautiful, unlike anything he'd seen in Ukraine or Russia. Its Habsburg architecture and layout, its cobblestone streets, were redolent of a different time and place. But, as the ugly high-rises reminded him once again, this too was the Soviet Union. Or had been. Or perhaps still was.

Bleary-eyed and unshaven, Bazarov knocked on the door of the Polish consulate. Despite a recent past involving pogroms on both sides, Poles and Ukrainians now claimed to love each other. The consulate serviced the substantial Polish minority that had resurfaced after the Soviet collapse. And it was indispensable to the thousands of Ukrainians who traveled to Poland to pick strawberries, clean sheds, work on constructions sites, and perform all manner of menial tasks that Poles deigned to do only further west—in Germany and France and Italy, but not at home.

The guard eyed him suspiciously, but after stating his case in Polish, Bazarov was ushered into the waiting room. Several minutes later a round-faced official walked in and asked Bazarov to accompany him to his office on the second floor. As the door closed and the official turned to him with a quizzical look on his face, Bazarov answered, "I am an American citizen. I must contact the Americans. Immediately."

CHAPTER 6

▼

Jane looked at her watch. They had been in the air for over one hour. Down below was in all likelihood Ukraine. How fitting, she thought, that I cannot see it, that it should be so very close and yet so very, very far. Am I closer to it now than in Long Island? Or was I closer to it then, when all they talked about was "home"? How can your home be thousands of miles away? How could you possibly retain all those connections to "home" even after having left it, surviving war and death, and doing everything possible to restart your life? By living here with your thoughts—that's how. That her baba and parents still thought of this place as home was not the mystery. Far more incredible is that *I* should not think of Long Island as home. That's where I was born, that's where I grew up. Our neighbors were just neighbors, never foreigners, to me. And yet, I have never felt at home there. Is that why I tried for the Agency? Because it promised to give me the opportunity to leave while pretending to retain my ties to a land that I never quite felt at home in or with? To be an émigré, almost a refugee, in the country of your birth would be astonishing. And this land below the cloud cover? What is it to me? A colored spot on a map populated by distant relatives who write and call, but whose lives and hopes and suffering could just as well be happening in Timbuktu. She remembered the first time she had traveled, as a graduate student, to Lviv in the Vienna-Moscow train. The sense of excitement as they approached the border town of Chop, the interminable wait as the train was lifted onto a differently gauged carriage, and the disappointment she sensed when she realized that she did not feel as if she were returning home. How strange it had been when her parents and grandmother would receive letters announcing so-and-so's death. They had cried, but she had felt nothing. And stranger still were the black and white photographs that accompanied the letters. There lay some woman, her face frozen, her head covered with a kerchief, her bed surrounded by mourners, the men all wearing dark suits and white shirts—always, for some reason, buttoned at the top—the women in dark skirts and dark sweaters and dark kerchiefs. The tableaux were always the same, regardless of who died and when. Ukraine seemed to be a place where some people only wrote letters containing little information about anything except their illnesses and others died, providing the dour-faced letter-writers with a pretext to don their Sunday best and stand awkwardly before cameras. Of course, sometimes they got married, but even then, the looks on their faces and the clothes they wore were the same as at funerals. Even the new-lyweds looked like they had gotten married in order to have something to write about in letters and something to talk about at funerals. Every once in a while Jane would also call, but she kept those verbal visitations to a minimum. There was so little to talk about. They told you about their illnesses and deaths, and what were you to say? That you had just gotten a job on Madison Avenue? That you had vacationed in the Bahamas? That the Yankees had won the pennant? That you had hopes for the future and expectations for the present? How do you talk to people without a past, without a present, and without a future?

Jane had last been in Kiev in the early nineties, during her posting in Berlin. She remembered that the American Embassy in Kiev used to be located in the ambassador's residence on Gorky Street, where the city's upper-crust Communists lived. But that was right after independence in 1991, when buying or renting a building was next to impossible in a country that still viewed private property as a historical aberration. Those were heady times. Ukrainians sincerely believed they'd become the France of the East within a few years, and Americans, persuaded that the end of history had come and that they could do anything—even transform wretched countries into flourishing democracies—rushed to the Soviet successor states with offers of technical assistance, investment, and expertise. Times had changed, in only a few years. Just about everyone she knew had given up on Ukraine. The France of the East threatened to become the Bangladesh of the West. The country was down the toilet, hopeless, hopelessly corrupt and hopelessly mismanaged and hopelessly headed for, as the Soviets used to put it, the ash heap of history. Or was it the garbage dump of history? Same thing, Jane thought, as her taxi clattered along Melnikov Street. The current embassy was a few kilometers from the city center and minutes away from Babi Yar, the ravine where—depending on whom you asked, the history book you read, or the monument you looked at—the Nazis had killed over one hundred thousand

Jews, or over one hundred thousand Jews, Ukrainians, and Russians, or over one hundred thousand Soviet citizens.

The flat white building—as obviously an embassy from its dull exterior as from the fence that surrounded it and the flag pole that adorned it—drew up on her left. She greeted the crisply dressed marine at the entrance—that, she thought, was the most telling difference between the two countries: American men had their pants and shirts pressed, Ukrainian men appeared not to know that irons existed—showed her papers, and walked inside. A long line of tired Ukrainians stood at the entrance to the consular section, hoping to get the tourist visas that would let them earn a few dollars as illegal laborers delivering pizza or painting houses in Cincinnati or Pittsburgh or New York. Naturally, the "new Ukrainians"—the *nouveaux riches* who made their money by stealing what they could before the population realized that privatization amounted to theft—had no trouble getting visas. They had bank accounts in Zürich, villas in Cyprus, summer homes in West Palm Beach, and friends in all the right places. Who held the future of this country in their hands—the people hoping to escape or the people expecting to steal? Some choice, she thought. Some country.

Her briefcase screened and an identification badge attached to her blouse, Jane took the elevator to the second floor and followed the antiseptic corridors—good God, I could be in Long Island. Why do Americans manage to recreate only the ugliest things about their country in foreign lands?—to the office of Robert Leppinger, her official counterpart, and the Agency's man, in Kiev. Why do we play this game? Everyone knows. Why not just openly announce that Smith is our man in Havana? If nothing else you could dispense with the ridiculous song and dance that only bureaucrats could possibly consider indispensable. It occurred to her that she should read Graham Greene again.

The door to his office was open. A young man, about thirty, in khaki pants and a blue button-down shirt—the sartorial antithesis of Bristol—rose from his desk and extended his hand.

"Bob," he said. "Bob Leppinger. Good to meet you, Jane. Coffee?"

Leppinger's office was small, consisting of two bookcases, a computer, and a large map of the Soviet Union pinned to the wall. Ukraine had been outlined with a red magic marker. Several issues of the *Kyiv Post*, the local English-language ex-pat newspaper, lay on his desk.

"Yes, thank you. Any news?" She pointed at the newspapers.

"Presidential elections," he said. "We have no milk. Will that powdered stuff do?" Leppinger handed her a Styrofoam cup and sat down. "I mean, if you can call a rigged election an election. But they say the opposition could win. Orange is their color. Don't know why."

"Everyone seems to be wearing it. Even my cabdriver."

"This town hates the official candidate." Leppinger leaned forward. "But he's going to win, of course. The president and his man control the process. The Russians control the president and his man. End of story."

"What's our policy?"

"We make sure none of our people gets killed. We track the whackos. We calm the Russians. We remind the president that fraud is no way to build democracy."

"That's *it*?"

"Yep," Leppinger said, rubbing his chin. "That's about it."

"Doesn't sound like much."

"Damn right it doesn't," he said. "But what else can we do? Kill the president? Kill the prime minister? Replace them with our own guys? Even if we could, the new guys would be no better. They're all corrupt bastards. I give this place ten years—max."

"Not exactly enamored of these people, are you?"

"They're sheep. These bastards are robbing them blind, and what do they do? Nothing.

"Anyway, it's probably better that way," he continued. "I mean, if you don't keep them down, they're liable to start a pogrom or something."

Leppinger stopped. "What's that you're reading?" he asked, pointing to the paperback in Jane's coat pocket.

"Spillane."

"Never heard of him. What is it? A romantic novel or something?"

"No, a mystery."

"Like James Bond?"

"Like the opposite of James Bond."

"What's the guy's name?"

"Mike Hammer."

"Some name." Leppinger whistled. "I bet he always gets the girl."

"He always gets *all* the girls."

"Screws them?"

"Kills them."

"Ouch. You like that stuff?"

"I'm a killer at heart," Jane said.

"Right. Whatever. Anyway," Leppinger, suddenly distracted, continued, "I'm glad you're here. Anything to break the routine." He reddened. "That didn't come out right. Sorry. I mean, it's so damned boring, you know?"

"No, I don't," Jane responded stiffly. "I'm at State, not the Agency."

"Same difference."

"Maybe." Jane felt a delicious pang of Schadenfreude. "You don't sound thrilled about this posting."

"Look. I'll level with you," Leppinger said. "The CIA was my Plan B. I failed the foreign service exam. Anyway, here I am, in fucking Kiev."

"Welcome to the club." Jane smiled. *Should I enjoy the irony or should I be bitter?* "I've been in the service for ten years and now they've got me running after some crazy professor."

"Yeah, I've been briefed. Looking for some guy named Bravarov, huh? A real operator, right?"

"Not much different from the other academics I've met," said Jane. "Except that he may be involved in money laundering."

"Wouldn't be the first time. And you figure his pals got bumped off because they were skimming some off the top?"

"Could be. What do you know about the Mir Foundation?"

"They have an affiliate here. Usual sort of place. You know, building institutions, building civil society, empowering women—that sort of thing. Oh, and don't forget building democracy."

"On the level?"

"Well, as on the level as any of these outfits. I mean, would you trust a Russian philanthropist? I always figured he's got some kind of side racket going."

"You know, Bazarov got ten million dollars for just that kind of project."

"Well," said Leppinger, his index finger raised, "that's big bucks for a bunch of academics, but it's minor league when it comes to money laundering. There are easier ways of getting dirty dollars into western banks."

"So why go to the trouble of setting up a foundation—"

"—unless, of course, that's not what the foundation is really up to. By the way, maybe it's on the level."

"I'm sure it is," said Jane, "or at least some of it is, but—"

"—but, in that case, why would these three guys get killed? Right?"

"Right, which is why—"

"—you're on this case. I know." Leppinger smiled. "Look, Jane, I've already done some poking around. Before you came." He pointed to a file on one of the bookshelves. "That affiliate of Mir. It's something called the Woman Institute.

Or is it the Women's Institute? Anyway, you might want to look into it. I mean, who knows? Right?"

"Right," said Jane. "Who knows? By the way, Leppinger—"

"Yes?"

"I need a rod."

"A what?"

"A rod. A gun. Can you get me one?"

"Do you know how to use one of those things, Jane?"

"Just get it."

Asshole, Jane thought, as she stormed out of the embassy. How the hell did we ever win the cold war? Not because we were better, but because they were so much worse. Their bureaucrats were even duller than ours—they *had* to be—and who knows what would have happened had ours been running the economy? Was the CIA any different? Jane remembered the Soviet agents she had met, both officially and unofficially. They had been smart, all of them. Smart and polished and clever and ruthless. One on one, they might've beaten us, especially if Leppinger wasn't the only one of his kind in the Agency. But with the ballast of impossibly stupid bureaucrats to drag them down, the KGB stood no chance. Now, even the ex-KGB agents had turned soft. The ones she knew in Vienna were all spies-turned-consumers, far more dedicated to sustaining their own indolence than fighting for Russia's power and glory. Perhaps Leppinger was symptomatic of the post-cold war doldrums that both spy agencies suffered from now that they had nothing to do? But who was she to criticize the spooks? Two years of drinking melanges and *Tees mit Zitrone* had taught her how to decipher obscure Viennese mannerisms and little else. And here I am, now, playing the hard-boiled dick in an awful country that claims to have some hold on a corner of my loyalty. I am looking for some silly professor, engaging mediocrities in conversation, and pretending that this is a career. But what's the alternative? Long Island?

The Institute was a single room, on the second floor of a tsarist-era building, with dirty windows, ratty rugs, a few metal cabinets, three desks, four chairs, one telephone, and four occupants, two men and two women. A woman, with bleached hair, was talking on the phone; the others were lounging about smoking cigarettes and laughing. As Jane walked in, one of the men looked up and said in Russian, "What do you want?" His brusqueness startled her.

"This—is this the Women's Institute?" she asked in English. "I was told that the Women's Institute is here."

"You are in right place," a red-haired woman said. "Who are you?"

"Jane Sweet. I represent the Long Island chapter of"—she paused momentarily—"the National Organization of Women. N.O.W."

"Now or never," said one of the men and grinned at the others.

"Yes, that's right. Now or never. We heard about you, about the work you're doing. From Professor Bazarov. Igor Bazarov. We'd like to know more. Maybe we can help. Maybe even work with you. Who knows?" Jane winced as she realized she had just used Leppinger's expression.

"Woman's Institute is just right partner for you," said the blonde. "We defend gender, help women in Ukraine, do training. We *beeld* civil society."

"And we empower females," added the redhead. "Against stupid Ukrainian men." She glared at the two men, who smiled back. "Excepting for Professor Bazarov, who is not stupid man."

"That's good," said Jane, "that's exactly what we at N.O.W. support. Could you tell me more about your programs? We'd be interested in inviting some Ukrainian women to America, have them work with us. Perhaps Professor Bazarov could help?"

"America is good," replied the blonde. "Many women go there. Many women go to Europe, too. We send women everywhere." She appeared to be looking at Jane's pants and shoes. "You want know what we really need?"

"What?"

"*Tek-nee-kahl ah-sees-tents.*"

"Yes, of course, I'm sure you do. But tell me. Where do these women go? Who are they?"

"Village women, city women, all classes, all nationalities. They go for training. In Europe—Vienna, Budapest, Berlin, Rome, Paris."

"For how long?"

"It's depending. One year, two year, three year. Program just begin."

"And who do they work for?"

"Civil society of Europe," replied the blonde. "Of course."

"Could you be more specific? In Vienna, for instance. Who do they work for in Vienna?"

"Mir Foundation. Very famous philanthropic society with excellent connection to civil society of Austria. You know Mir?"

"Yes. And Professor Bazarov? What does he do for you?"

"Igor Alexandrovich is best man in world."

The phone rang and the blonde lifted the receiver. "*Allo,*" she said. There seemed to be no response. "*Allo, allo. Da, eto ya.* Yes, it's me. *Da,* I'm listening." She placed her forefinger to her lips and the others fell silent. The redhead lit a cigarette, the two men watched the blonde, and Jane, uncertain of what to do, made as if to rise from her chair. The blonde, with one swift wave of her hand, motioned her to remain seated.

"*Da,*" she said. "*Da.*" Another pause followed by another *da.* Finally, after a string of *da*'s, she replaced the receiver.

"Sergei, Boris," she turned to the two men. "*Poshli.* Let's go."

She looked at Jane. "Natasha, stay here with our guest. And Jane—I may say you Jane?—stay with Natasha."

The blonde slipped on a red leather jacket and, with the two men in tow, left the office. Jane looked at the redhead named Natasha. Her thin hair was cut short, and she wore a brown skirt, black stockings, a brown blouse, and a black sweater with an orange pin.

"You want coffee?" she asked.

"No, thank you."

"Maybe cognac?"

"No," Jane said. "Oh, sure, why not."

"You come first time to Kiev?"

"Yes." Jane took a sip. It was, she noticed by the plastic top on the bottle, some cheap Georgian brand.

"You from America?"

"New York."

"I never was there. Maybe you invite me?"

"Hasn't Professor Bazarov ever invited you?"

"Me? No. Only Seryozha and Borya. They go to New York all time."

"The two men who were just here?"

The redhead nodded. "They very active. They building institutes everywhere."

"Women's institutes?"

"*Da.*"

"Where?"

"There where are Ukrainian women."

"Let me guess," said Jane, recalling that Turks called the Russian-speaking prostitutes of Istanbul Natashas. "In Istanbul?"

The redhead nodded.

"Tel Aviv?"

Another nod.

"Berlin, *natürlich*."

Natasha said nothing.

"And, of course, Brighton Beach."

"There is big office," said Natasha. "There is beautiful, yes?"

"Very," said Jane. "They call it 'Little Odessa'."

"It is port?"

"No, just a beach, with a boardwalk and an elevated train."

"Everyone there is Ukrainian, yes?"

"Ukrainian, Russian, Jewish," said Jane.

"Igor Alexandrovich, he tell us of nightclubs, dancing there."

"That's what I hear."

"Igor Alexandrovich is owner of club. I think name is Good Time."

"Really?"

"Oh, yes," gushed Natasha. "Igor Alexandrovich is best man in world."

"You're in luck, Jane," Leppinger said, as she walked into his office. "By the way, how was your visit to the ladies' institute?"

"What is it?"

Leppinger shuffled among the papers that had accumulated on his desk since their meeting. "Now where is it?" he murmured. "Ah!" he cried. "This came in, a fax, from some fellow named Bristol. From Vienna." Leppinger handed her a sheet of paper.

Our friend Zabarov, read the fax, *appears to be hiding in the Polish consulate in Lvov. He called this morning, requesting help. The chief thinks you should go there, pronto. Good luck.* Jane read the document several times. How could Bristol compose something this fatuous? How could he send it by fax? Was there no end to his stupidity? And that *pronto*. He didn't just speak that way: he actually wrote that way! Incredulous, she raised her eyes from the paper and caught Leppinger's grin.

"Sorry," he said, "couldn't help reading it. Not exactly following procedures, your friend."

"No," she replied acidly, "and neither are you."

"Couldn't be helped, though I know what you mean. My secretary, Lenochka, brought me the fax. She knew you had been here to see me."

"How did she know? Did you tell her?"

"Well, no. I guess she must have seen you."

"Is the fax machine secure?"

"Well, no," Leppinger mumbled. "I mean, yes. It's in the embassy, isn't it?"

So now the killer also knew of Bazarov's whereabouts. The locals who staffed American embassies were screened and checked and cross-checked, but everyone knew that a good number of them were working for somebody else—hostile governments, friendly governments, transnational corporations, criminal organizations, you name it. The cold war might be over, but espionage was still big business. Especially in places like these—where your salary, even if in dollars, just barely helped make ends meet—the temptation to make a few bucks on the side could be overwhelming. Especially if all you had to do was report on some visitor or conversation or phone call—or fax.

A UkraineAir flight to Lviv departed in two hours. She asked Leppinger to get her an embassy car and call the airport to reserve a seat. He promptly got on the phone and barked some commands. When he finished speaking, he turned to Jane, his face red.

"I'm sorry," he stammered. "I guess I fucked up."

Jane said nothing. What do you say to an asshole? Instead, she reached into her pocket and tossed the Spillane onto Leppinger's desk.

"Read it," she said. "Maybe you'll learn something." Five minutes later, their parting glances averted and a bulge in her purse, Jane left Leppinger standing at the embassy gate and climbed into the black Cadillac at the curb.

Jane's seat was at the back of the plane, an old Ilyushin that barely got off the ground and just managed to clear the trees. It rocked from side to side, even after they rose above the clouds. Was the pilot drunk? She knew that Soviet pilots thought that a glass of vodka steadied the nerves and improved concentration. Why not this one? The seat belts didn't lock. The passengers around her didn't seem to care. Their packages lay strewn about, unsecured. Some smoked, others pulled out bottles of vodka and began drinking just as the useless seat belt sign went off. The stewardesses distributed little plastic trays covered with a transparent plastic wrap. A pair of cold frankfurters, a dab of yellowing mustard, a slice of black bread, and a plastic knife stared out from beneath the glossy covering. Jane's neighbors didn't seem to care, eating the sausages between shots of vodka. She felt nauseous. What's the matter with this place? Or is it just me? Why can't I appreciate local color anymore? A dark-haired man in a black leather jacket and jeans offered her a glass. For a second Jane hesitated. Then she quickly downed the whole glass—to the roaring approval of her neighbors. The man poured her another glass, and she promptly drank that one too.

"*Vy nasha?*" he asked. "Are you one of us?"

"My parents are Ukrainian," she said hesitantly. "I'm from America."

"*Vy nasha!*" he cried triumphantly. "*Absolyutno nasha.*"

"Well, maybe not absolutely," she countered weakly. She felt the alcohol going to her head.

"*Ni, ni,*" the man said. "*Absolyutno! Absolyutno!*"

"Well, then, I guess it's *absolyutno,*" she said—and immediately fell asleep.

Snippets of conversation, the ramblings of two old women, the incoherent mutterings of baba and mama. They board the ship in the evening. The gangway creaks every time mama takes a tentative step. The filthy water swirls beneath her feet. Horses neigh. The air is heavy with the smell of clams. Baba meets her at the top of the gangway, holding Stefan and Slava by their hands. Come, she says gently, come. Our cabin is below. Loud voices, nervous laughter, and the clatter of shoes surround her. Her father is dead, in the burial grounds far from Fall River's immigrant neighborhoods, far from their street. The mirror in the living room falls and shatters in the night. That is a bad sign. The next day he dies. Her father is dead, her father has been transported on a horse-drawn carriage, through the snow and wind, to be deposited in the burial grounds. The mirror has crashed, forewarning them of his death. Her mother has dried her eyes as she sits impassively in the carriage, holding the children and wondering.

The waves slam against the side of the boat. The three children huddle in the beds, their mother snores. Sailors run along the deck. In the cabin next door, several Germans are playing cards and drinking beer. She awakes. The room is dark. Cigarette smoke slides through the cracks. It is their neighborhood in the evening. Her mother sitting on the front stoop, the Portuguese and Polish women exchanging gossip, the men arguing and playing cards, the children in shorts on the street, the dark-haired Gypsies, the smell of snails, broken beer bottles in the alley, a train passing in the distance, the ragman with the cap pulled over his eyes.

A terrible storm catches the ship, slamming it, shaking it, pulling it down and, just at the point when it seems to be under water, letting it go. The waves are as tall as houses, the wind whistles mad songs. She lies in bed, clasping its sides with all her might, praying to Jesus and Mary, praying that this terrible fury might end. Stefan is asleep, oblivious to the war. Slava is lying in her mother's arms, her soft sobs barely audible. She lies in bed, praying, thinking of the ocean when it was calm, when the waves slapped the boat playfully, when gulls appeared from nowhere and trailed the ship, suspended in the air like kites. The ship lurches. The roar of the ocean frightens her, and she clenches the cross more tightly.

The ocean is quiet today, and all the children are playing on deck. Rusty freighters with unpronounceable names pass the boat every few hours. Seagulls glide in the back, their lonely cries disrupting the children's shrieks. A ball rolls along the deck and comes to a stop at her feet. She stands at the railing, leaning over, watching the foam appear and disappear. The horizon is all around her. Her legs shiver. The salty air makes it hard to breathe. There is nothing but water all around. She has never seen anything like this. She leads her brother to the cabin by the hand. Their mother leans against the railing and peers at the ocean.

The ship looks tiny on the ocean, surrounded by snow-capped mountains. The toy boat is shoved from side to side, spray explodes around it, waves inundate it, push it into the salty water, keeping its head down until it can barely breathe and then letting go. The boat rises and falls and rises and falls, and with it her mind goes in circles, her hands clasp the picture of the Virgin, her eyes are closed, her lips mutter a prayer, over and over and over again as if the repetition, the mere repetition of words, would stop nature, halt the movement of the stars, and turn back the force of the ocean. The boat is traveling in darkness, the waves are beating the sides ominously, the clouds have gathered, the sun remains hidden.

Jane awoke with a start. The plane seemed to have fallen to the ground. Her head spinning, her stomach queasy, she looked at her companions. They were all snoring and they remained asleep even as the plane came to a halt somewhere in the middle of the runway. Where was she? The passenger cabin signified a plane, but the memory of the ship remained far more vivid than the pale reality. It was only after the man who had insisted she was "absolutely one of them" rubbed his eyes awake and smiled at her that she realized where she was.

"L'viv," he pointed through the window, pronouncing the "L" softly. "*Evropa.*"

A battered blue and yellow bus drove the passengers to the terminal, a preposterous Stalinist structure with a gilded cupola, frescoes of noble peasants and proletarians, marble columns, and—as Jane immediately noticed upon stepping into the main hall—the pungent smell of sweat, so reminiscent, it suddenly occurred to her, of France. She caught a taxi and instructed the unshaven driver to take her to the *Zhorzh*—the Hotel George, an elegant old-world structure built in Habsburg days that the Soviets, despite their best efforts, had never fully managed to destroy. Thoroughly renovated, it now stood proudly between the monument to Poland's great national poet, Adam Mickiewicz, and a glistening McDonald's.

The driver negotiated the alarmingly uneven streets with great dexterity, swerving to the left, then to the right, in order to avoid the avoidable potholes, indentations, and protruding tram tracks. The unavoidable obstacles shook and rattled the beaten old car, forcing it to slow down to some five miles per hour. The driver emitted occasional curses at the pedestrians, all seemingly in a hurry and all oblivious to the traffic. The men were all short, their hair cropped close, cigarettes protruding from their lips, their shirts white and buttoned to the top, their suits—amazingly, Jane thought, they're all wearing suits—invariably dark, almost as invariably striped, their black shoes dirty. Just as in the photographs. The older women sported shapeless dresses, usually with floral patterns—yes, exactly the kind baba used to wear—their heads covered with equally flowery scarves. The younger women were obviously trying to be Western, or what would have passed for Western two decades ago, preferring excruciatingly short mini-skirts, tight jeans, and high heels. All were partial to henna and purplish eyeliner and mascara. Jane looked at herself and her clothes: they'll know immediately that I'm a foreigner.

She had been in Lviv several times, before she had joined State and during her tour of duty in Berlin and Bucharest. It was then that she had met the countless relatives, who descended on her from the city as well as a score of towns and villages that she barely recalled from baba's conversations with her parents. Except for the mechanical phone calls on exceedingly rare occasions, she had lost touch with all of them—or almost all of them. One distant cousin, Arkady, occasionally wrote letters in awkward English and she would respond, never quite knowing what to say to someone who could just as easily have been living on the dark side of the moon. The correspondence, although infrequent, continued to this day.

The first time she met Arkady was in the seventies, in her hotel room. He was intense and intelligent, with sharp dark eyes and a slight smile. He opened a bottle of vodka, and they drank. The room was bugged, but they didn't care. They talked about various things—she no longer remembered what—but mostly they drank, shot after shot, until the bottle was empty and they were embracing and calling each other brother and sister. Downstairs, the lobby was full of relatives, aunts and uncles and first cousins and second cousins and their children. They walked through the city, a caravan of stubby old peasant men and women and bored children and curious young people, with their flowery skirts and uncreased pants, and their unpolished black shoes and violet lipstick.

The taxi pulled up at the entrance to the *Zhorzh*. A burly doorman dressed in a tight-fitting red suit opened the door and extended his hand. She stepped out, noticing the look of disappointment that crossed his face as he saw her pant-cov-

ered legs. The lobby was shabby, but it no longer had the feel of Soviet misman-
agement. This may have been what the hotel looked like in the last days of the
Habsburgs—a provincial oasis for the aristocrats and priests fleeing the war and
communism. Her room was on the third floor, in the back. She breathed a sigh of
relief when she saw that the windows overlooked a quiet street, and not the
McDonald's.

There was no avoiding what she knew she had to do. She picked up the
receiver and dialed Arkady's number. After six rings—she had told herself that
she would hang up after the seventh—his voice broke in with an *allo*. Funny,
how their way of saying hello makes you feel as if you're imposing on them.

"It's Jane, Arkady. Jane Sweet."

"Ivanka! Ivanka Svit! Where are you?"

"Here in Lviv. On business."

"You come visit us?"

"I can't, Arkady, I can't. I don't have time this time. I'm sorry." This was
always the worst part—the refusal and the silence that followed.

"Arkady?" she continued. "How are you?" Or was this the worst part—the
question that always led to a long lamentation and a feeling of overpowering
powerlessness?

"Same. I was in hospital. Medicaments are no good."

"And how are the others?" she asked weakly. *Which* others?

"Roman—"

"Your son?"

"Roman broke last winter leg."

"Is he better?"

"You remember Ivan, my brother? He have automobile accident."

"Is he OK?"

"He is fixing car. Accident was not his fault."

Stop, Arkady, please stop.

"Ivan have bad stomach," Arkady said, almost as an afterthought.

"Is he taking medicine?"

"All time. But it no good. What you can do?"

What you can do?

"Arkady," Jane said, "Arkady, I have to go now. But I'll call again. And you
write. OK?"

"I pray for you," he said and hung up.

What you can do?

What you can do?

Oh, what you can do?

Her body numb, Jane sank into the bed. She couldn't sleep. She recalled the time they had visited their grandfather's grave. It was August and they drove. They reached the city around noon. Having no idea where he was buried, they methodically combed through two large Catholic cemeteries near the center of town. No, said her mother, it's not here. This is too big. There were no other cemeteries on the map. But just beyond the bridge they found a tiny rectangle: it didn't even have the little crosses that signified a cemetery. An immigrant wouldn't have been laid to rest among the grandiose monuments of the Bordens and Fall River's other elites. Simple burial grounds would have been just fine. He lay there among Polish and Portuguese names, a few feet from a chain-link fence, which stood a few feet from a row of wooden clap-board houses, with white laundry flapping in the wind.

There was much to remember, so much to arrange and rearrange, so much to make sense of, so many chapters of her life to be written and rewritten. Too much, too many.

There was, she remembered, the cemetery in Lviv. She had walked along the winding paths, among the trees, between the gravestones, reading the inscriptions, the years of birth, the years of death. The air had smelled of wet grass, poppies, and old leaves. Here lies a beloved father, there a beloved wife. Children, one year old, two years old, three years old, lie next to their parents. An angel, a look of anguish on his weather-beaten face, stands above a grave, his right arm draped over the stone, his left hanging at his side. *Oy, yak to bolyt'*, says the inscription. Oh, how it hurts. There was, she remembered, the window in Vienna, overlooking the street where the prostitutes gathered at night. She looked out at the lengthening shadows, a hot breeze caressed her eyelids, her lips half closed, her thoughts on yesterday evening and the evening to come. There was the doorway near the Sperl, the faded ochre and orange and white forming the perfect backdrop for her profile, head raised slightly, nose aloft, her eyes smiling, half facing forward, half looking at the camera, her left hand resting decorously on her bosom. There was the wine garden in Grinzing, the setting sun, the languorous shadows, the clear wine magnifying the sparkle in her eyes. There was the Alpine inn on Mount Rax. A rough wooden table near the window, to the left a cliff, in front and to the right rocks and low, thick, thorny bushes. Patches of grass, green and then blue and finally gray. The heavy-set waiter, another round of glasses, shouts of *prosit*, laughter, pointing, mountain goats. There were other chapters, so many other chapters. Singing in Berlin's *Kneipen*, dancing and drinking, crossing the border, living in one-room flats, slapping backs, dancing waltzes, ordering espressos, sniffing beers, polishing shoes, knotting ties, salting soups, eating, drinking, laughing, dancing, walking, talking, standing, sitting, lying.

Wait, Jane thought. The order of the narrative wasn't quite right. Perhaps it would be best to make the first chapter second, the second fourth, and the fourth first? Or the fourth second, the second first, and the first fourth? But what of the third chapter? Should the third stay third or should it be moved into the first, second, or fourth slots? That meant twenty-four different versions. But how could that be? How could there be twenty-four similar, yet different, versions of the same life? Wasn't the point to choose—to produce the one best possible narrative? But how was she to do that? What if she just imagined one big chapter? That way the problem of different permutations resolved itself automatically, didn't it? Only if you considered the problem in terms of chapters. Once you descended to the level of paragraphs and sentences and words and even letters, then what seemed at first glance to be a solution was, in reality, just an infinitely more complicated version of the original problem. How many paragraphs would she need? How many sentences? How many words? How many letters? The mathematics was beyond her comprehension. She knew only that the numbers would prove to be so huge as to be completely, utterly, absolutely beyond her ability to cope with them. There was nothing to be done; there was no way out of this *cul de sac*. She recalled a nightmare she had as a child: trapped on the Titanic and forced to add immensely long columns of numbers. The panic, the fear, the blackness, the impenetrability of the numbers, their weight, their ubiquity. Numbers had always scared her, especially the fact that there was no limit to them. They went on and on, and even the spaces between numbers consisted of infinite gradations of numbers. She recalled that there were supposed to be some fifty billion galaxies in the universe. Was the figure accurate or only an estimate? Perhaps the real number was only forty-eight billion? Or forty-six? What difference did a billion or two make? What difference did it make just how the narrative was ordered? Wasn't the point that it made no difference? Wasn't the point that it was the narrative, and not its ordering, that made the difference? Was that fatalism or fate?

Jane opened her eyes. I need a drink, she said aloud and sat upright in the darkened room. She put on a dress and a pair of pumps, combed her hair, applied some of the purple lipstick she had bought in the lobby, and made her way to the bar. Except for the gray-haired man with a mustache, the place was empty. She sat three stools down from him and ordered a cognac and an espresso.

"It's a beautiful hotel now," she said to the bartender.

"*Da,*" he replied and turned away to wash the glasses. Jane began sipping her cognac, paused while holding the glass to her lips, and then downed the liquid. The gray-haired man was smiling as she put down the glass.

"You are not from here," he said quietly. His English was perfect.

"Is it that obvious?"

"Ukrainian women know how to drink. You do not. But you are trying. I commend you."

"I'm from the States," Jane said. "Ukrainian background though. I'm here visiting family."

"I have been to America," he said. "I am Russian, a filmmaker. I am here to do a film about the city. Do you know it?"

"Not well. My relatives have never let me."

"Then I will show it to you," he said. "If you like."

Jane nodded. Why not? Why not have some fun on this wretched assignment?

"My name is Jane Sweet," she said. "The Ukrainian is Svit. Ivanka Svit."

"A real pleasure, Miss Jane Sweet," the man said. "Anatoly Sergeevich Filatov at your service."

CHAPTER 7

▼

It dawned upon him during the flight just how much he dreaded returning to this city. Lvov—the city of his boyhood, the city that killed his parents and destroyed his innocence, the city that drove him to seek refuge in the secret police, the city that, in the final analysis, was responsible for the collapse of the Soviet Union, the collapse of communism, and the collapse of Anatoly Filatov. And now that the war is over—Lvov won and I lost—I am returning, almost in penance, to the place that rejected me. What a savage irony. The whiskey priest embarks on his Canossa. To seek redemption? To seek forgiveness? To seek revenge? To lay down his life—for what? For the cause? For what cause? There is no cause. There is no war, no battle, no fight anymore.

How much simpler things had been when the fighting had ended and the fascists had been defeated, when his father returned from the front and collected his family. Filatov remembered his sudden appearance. They had not heard from him for several years, his mother had assumed that he had been killed, and then, one fall day as the weather had turned especially crisp, a bedraggled man appeared on their doorstep. Filatov had run away upon seeing him, but his mother broke into tears and threw her arms around the emaciated stranger she called Seryozha. They walked and talked for days, his mother holding the strange thin man tightly around his waist, his arm drooped awkwardly about her shoulders. His long coat, stained and dirty, swept the grass as they walked. When they ate, they sat in silence at the table, his father methodically breaking off pieces of dark bread, dipping them into the beet soup or wiping them against the pan to soak up the fat. His mother watched him, her eyes lowered. At night the talking would resume. The boy would lie on the cot near the stove, arrange his sweater, coat, and fur hat, and cover himself up to his ears with the remnants of a blanket. It was impossible not to hear—crickets, an occasional dog, and his father's voice muffled by his mother's tears.

The Lithuanian fascists almost killed me, Nadia. It was a miracle that I escaped. Oh, Seryozha! Our forces were gone. Soviet bodies lay among the tall grasses. German tanks pounded eastward. Black smoke rose above the horizon. Men with thick accents distributed leaflets and waved Luger pistols. Columns of dusty prisoners drifted along the roads. There was chaos in the town. Boys tore down the red flags. Mobs ran through the streets looking for our people. I hid in the prison cellar. Yells, the rush of heavy footsteps. The door was crashed open. There he is, someone shouted. Kill the red, kill him, they screamed. I pressed my back to the cellar wall. Hands grabbed me by the collar. Fists hit my face. I felt blood trickling down my chin. As they pulled me by my arms, feet kicked my thighs. A stick struck the side of my head. They pushed me into the street. I stumbled and fell. Communist pig, Soviet pig, they cried. A stone hit me in the eye. Kill the Soviets, someone cried, kill the Communists. They dragged me to the town square, near the burning synagogue. The women spat at me. The men kicked me. Communist pig, Soviet pig, they cried. I covered my face with my hands.

His mother wails; his father says, be quiet, Nadia, you'll wake Tolya.

We sat in dark malodorous wagons, he whispers. There is no emotion in his voice; he speaks in a quiet monotone, and the boy must strain his ears and his eyes in order not to be lulled to sleep. Bright light filtered through the cracks. We sat silently, motionlessly. The crackling straw, the rhythm of the train, occasional coughs and curses. Where were the fascist barbarians? That was the only thought in our minds. When the train stopped in Kursk, we streamed out, some to the latrines, some to smoke, most just gasping for air. Village women, huddled in the corners, their children asleep at their feet. I chewed on a piece of black bread I had in my pocket. Oh, how thin you still are, Seryozha, says his mother. You are all skin and bones. Quiet, says his father, be quiet, Nadia, you'll wake Tolya. And then, back on the train, back on the train, the sergeants shouted. We rode through the night, each of us claiming a spot on the floor, the cold night air blowing through the cracks, the steady rhythm of the train, the sight of blurred stars rushing past us, rushing west, while we moved east. We arrived in Voronezh late next day. The train pulled into the station, the doors slid open, the sergeants ordered us to climb out, to get in file. We marched out. The people were silent, scurrying along the streets, holding their children tightly by the hand. Leafy trees lined the streets. The boy falls asleep, fading images of leafy streets dancing in his mind.

When his father fell out of bed one night, he remained on the floor, shivering, motionless, slipping in and out of sleep, barely breathing, barely exhaling, his mouth half open. His mother found him in the morning, curled like a child, whimpering. Wake up, she said, you are on the floor, wake up. He had lost much weight, but when she and the boy tried pulling him up, she had to strain every muscle in her thick legs. Sleep, she whispered, as she covered him. Would you like something to eat, would you? His face remained quiet, his mouth closed. Where are your eyes? Where is your mouth? Where has your face gone? Can you still laugh? Can you even smile? Will you ever eat what I cook for you?

A few months later his father was posted to the territories recently annexed to the Soviet motherland. Somewhere in the west, somewhere past the steppes and wheat fields, somewhere the great Stalin had just liberated from the capitalist yoke. Filatov remembered the apartment they occupied in the center of the city. The ceilings were higher than anything he had ever seen. The walls were smooth and covered with moldings that reminded him of photographs of the inside of the Kremlin. The windows were over two meters high, and there was a porcelain bathtub in the house and a toilet in the hallway. The bathtub was an astonishing thing, spotlessly white during the day, but filled at night with cockroaches of all sizes, running, standing still, grazing like sheep. When he turned on the lights, they scurried about madly, some around the insides of the tub, some trying to climb out. They disgusted him, and to touch one would have been unthinkable, but to tease them, to hunt them was a sport, a war.

The most astonishing thing of all was that the apartment was overflowing with dressers and chairs and tables and sofas and beds and stools and glasses and cups and plates and forks and knives made of silver. The great Stalin had provided for everything. Even the drawers were full of diaphanous gowns he had never seen before. Some of the shirts and pants and skirts were too large, some too small, but, after a few expert adjustments by his mother, all could be easily made to fit. He remembered how the family would stroll along Lenin Boulevard dressed in their fancy clothes.

He remembered his father's uniform and he remembered wondering why he never wore it to work. Why leave such a beautiful outfit hanging in the closet? Why not let the neighbors know that he was important? Many of his friends' fathers wore their uniforms proudly. They walked with their heads held high, their chests extended, their medals glistening in the sun. They walked as triumphant warriors, as members of the world's greatest army—the Red Army, which had single-handedly defeated the fascist hordes led by that ridiculous little Hitler. That stupid-looking man was no match for the great Stalin, the remarkable Iosef Vissarionovich Stalin, the Generalissimo of the invincible Soviet armed forces, the man who led the brave Soviet workers and peasants to victory, the man who conquered Berlin and who would have killed Hitler with his bare hands, had not the German coward taken his own life. Why did his father not dress like these warriors? Why did he don some tattered old suit, leave his hair unwashed, and go to work before daybreak and return only after sunset? Sitting in the taxi, Filatov involuntarily smiled at his own innocence.

Life was good. There was always food on the table, anything you wanted. He slept in a real bed with a real mattress. The apartment was unusually bright, almost as if you were outside. Only the hallway was dark. The toilet, which stood near the staircase, smelled of cigarette smoke, but that didn't bother him. He took aim at the butts in the toilet bowl and tried to break them in half. They were warships and he was a Soviet aviator. His father and his friends played cards, smoked, and drank vodka in the room farthest from the kitchen, the one facing the street. Once, he came up to the table, and Colonel Vassilev said, Here, have a drink. And he did. He swallowed the shot of vodka and ran to the kitchen, his throat burning. His father and the other men laughed.

Then everything changed. The strolls on Lenin Boulevard became less frequent and shorter. His father returned home one evening with cuts and bruises on his faces, but his mother, who usually flew into a rage whenever he got too drunk, said nothing. His friends' fathers stopped strutting about in their uniforms, except on official occasions. Everyone seemed to have become nervous, everyone seemed to want to hide. But from what? His father said that the "German-Ukrainian bourgeois nationalists" were at fault, but what was a German-Ukrainian bourgeois nationalist? He had never seen one. Until the day he did. It was spring and he was playing in the courtyard of a friend's house. Two young men in bulky coats climbed the stairs. A few minutes later they emerged from the stairwell and ran into the street. As he heard his friend's mother scream, the boys ran up the stairs and burst through the door. His friend's father was slumped over his desk, an axe in the back of his head, his books and papers splattered with blood.

"Who killed Yaroslav Bogdanovich?" he asked his father.

"The German-Ukrainian bourgeois nationalists."

"But who are they?"

"They are lackeys of Hitler."

"What do they want?"

"To kill Comrade Stalin."

"What horrible people."

Just how horrible was brought home to him several months later, in the fall. His father had said that they should put on their fanciest clothes, that they would stroll down the boulevards and go to a fine restaurant to celebrate the anniversary of the Great October Socialist Revolution. As they turned off Zelenaya Street into a narrow alley, he remembered hearing footsteps—his father paused and began to turn in their direction—followed by explosions. He could still see his parents, lying on their faces, the cobblestones beneath them slowly turning red.

As the taxi rumbled along the streets, Filatov's gaze fell upon the ubiquitous blue and yellow flag—the banner of the victorious nationalists. He knew now that they had been worthy foes of Soviet power. It had been a vicious war. They had fought nobly and well, but we had won—then, in the fifties. Now, it was they who were victorious. We thought we had won the war, but we had only won a series of battles. In 1991, they had won the war—unconditionally. Worse, we had lost the war, ignobly, without resistance, without so much as firing a shot. We had simply thrown down our weapons and run. The nationalists never gave up. You had no choice but to kill them or ship them off to Siberia. But we just walked out of our offices, put on new clothes, and pretended that eighty years of communism had never happened. Fittingly, the large statue of Lenin in front of the Opera was gone. Not even the outline of the pedestal remained.

He told the driver to make a detour down Zelenaya.

"You mean Zelena," he said in Ukrainian. "Unless you want to walk back to Russia."

"*Nyet*, I mean, *ni*," replied Filatov in Ukrainian, "Zelena. Please take me to Zelena."

One hour later Filatov checked into the hotel. The manager asked him if he was feeling well, but Filatov replied that he had had a long journey and needed to lie down. You must have flown with UkraineAir, the manager joked, but you'll be able to find something in the minibar to calm your nerves. Filatov smiled weakly and took the elevator to his floor. His hands were trembling as he opened the door. He dumped his bags, threw off his clothes, grabbed a beer, and climbed into the bathtub. As the hot water rose to his chest, he opened the bottle and took a long drink.

Was it Volodya who taught him that trick? They had been friends in Moscow, where they wandered the back streets of the city, drank wine, and talked about girls. If you're ever attacked, Volodya once said in a bar, here's what you do. He led Filatov outside and broke the beer bottle against the side of the building. See this jagged edge? If you shove it into someone's face, he'll be scarred for life. I could do the same, thought Filatov, right now. He extended his left arm and looked at the veins lining his arm. A quick cut here and there, and it could all be over in a few minutes. The water would turn red, my head would feel giddy—would I become, as Comrade Stalin put it, giddy with success?—my arms and legs would appear to float, and as the water became hotter and sweat poured down my face, the rest of my body would turn colder. Until it became quite cold, and that would be that. Filatov finished the bottle. He climbed out of the tub and lay down naked on the bed.

We Marxists used to say that the state would wither away, but instead that fate has befallen my world. The irony was almost delicious. I was once alive, fully alive in a fully living world. And now I am dead. I do not recall any one moment when the world suddenly turned dark or when I suddenly lost my soul. It is as if a sliver of life escaped me every day. When I risked my life, when the world seemed to crash down on me and my comrades, I was alive. But the war is over, and I feel dead. I am a veteran. For years I sat in the trenches, I slept in the trenches, I endured the constant pounding of the guns, I ran through barbed wire with a rifle in my hand, my heart beating, the shrapnel flying, my comrades falling. I lived in mud, I stood in water, I slept with rats. The war is over, and I am lost. I miss the trenches. I miss the pockmarked fields, the dead trees, the whistling rockets.

"*Der Alltag tötet*," a West German comrade used to say. "Everyday life kills." We had just pulled off a successful *Aktion* against the imperialists. None of us had been caught or killed. We retreated and regrouped in a large apartment on the edge of the city. Some had argued against renting such luxurious quarters, but I had said that it would look suspicious if eight people suddenly appeared in a tiny one-room apartment. We had no choice, I had said, and I was right. But I was right only in this one respect: that we had no choice but to rent a large apartment. Otherwise, we chose all the time. We exercised our freedom every day and every minute of every day. If to be alive is to choose, if to be human is to choose, then we were as alive and as human as could possibly be. Andreas and I spent many hours talking, especially in the immediate aftermath of some *Aktion*. Both of us felt the onrush of depression, of the spiritual death portended by the *Alltag*, and we found that we could delay that dreaded moment by talking about the freedom we had experienced before and during the *Aktion*. We went through the steps of planning and executing the *Aktion* minutely. We discussed everything: how and why we had decided to do this and not that, how and why we had decided to approach the target by this street in this kind of vehicle, and escape by that street and that kind of vehicle. What we would say, to whom, and with what tone of voice, and then what we actually did say, to whom, and with what tone of voice. We relived the *Aktion* in every single detail. We constructed "what if?" scenarios. What if the light had not turned green at that precise moment? What would we have done? Would we have run the red light? What if the terrified woman with the motherly face had screamed? Would we have shot her? Or would we have tried to comfort her, perhaps even stroked her face and wiped away her tears? What if a comrade had been shot? Would we have left him or shot him or helped him up? We knew that there were no definitive answers to these questions, but that was exactly why we relished pursuing them. They gave us an infinite number of choices to make, and after arguing about why we would choose this over that, we could make the choice and then argue about the next scenario, and the next one. The *Aktion* continued to live, and the moment of reckoning—when the *Alltag* would finally descend upon and envelope us—could be delayed.

We often talked about the nature of time. Andreas once said that time kills, that time is the *Alltag*. An *Aktion*, he said, stops time; it kills the *Alltag*. The Wall also stopped time. It cut it in half and threw the parts away. The Wall defeated time. You could sense that most palpably if you stood in the middle of no-man's land. There, time did not exist. You were who you were, you lived, you died, you chose, you chose not to choose, you were human. Everything was possible in no-man's land. The Wall made everything possible, because it made us free, completely, terrifyingly free. Freedom is in the trenches, where you stand in waste-high mud, where bombs explode around you, where shrapnel whizzes past your eyes, where rats eat your food. It is in no-man's land, where you run through the barbed wire, jump over the craters, your rifle in your hand, your heart pounding, your comrades falling. "*Der Alltag tötet*," Andreas said, and he was right, absolutely right. It may not immediately destroy the body, but it does much worse. It destroys the mind, the soul, and the heart. It captures us, twists us, squeezes us, smothers us. When it is through with us, we are nothing, not human, not good, not evil.

Filatov felt cold. It was time to go to work—his lamentable excuse for an *Aktion*. He dressed slowly, meticulously knotting his tie, combing his hair and mustache, and polishing his shoes. A few minutes later he went down to the hotel bar.

It was empty. He sat on one of the stools and ordered a hundred grams of vodka and a Fanta. The bartender was busy with the glasses. The waitresses occasionally peeked in and flirted with him. Filatov downed the vodka and took a long sip of the soda. He ordered another hundred grams.

A woman walked in. A blonde, of medium height, wearing a tight-fitting dress. She looked around uncertainly and, after some hesitation, approached the bar, seating herself three stools away. She ordered a cognac and coffee and tried to start a conversation with the bartender. Despite the purple lipstick, it was obvious that she was the American.

After Filatov paid for the drinks, they crossed into the restaurant and took a corner table. The folk décor—down to the embroidered tablecloths—was completely at odds with the stately Habsburg interior. A desultory waiter watched them from behind a large plant. Jane was surprised to see that Filatov held the chair for her. He was equally surprised to see that she did not, contrary to his expectations, object.

"Shall we start with vodka or cognac?" he asked.

"Let's have both," said Jane, much to her own amazement.

The waiter brought two bottles, one of Ukrainian vodka and another of Armenian brandy, along with a one-liter bottle of Carpathian mineral water and two bottles of beer.

"To you, Miss Jane Sweet," said Filatov. "May you have a long and healthy life."

After they drank, the waiter brought the salads. Notwithstanding the different names he assigned to each, they appeared to Jane to be identical concoctions of chopped-up vegetables and huge amounts of mayonnaise. Even Viennese cuisine wasn't this unremittingly heavy.

"You are making a film, Mr. Filatov?"

"Yes. About Lviv. And you are visiting relatives?" He said *Lviv*, she thought, not Lvov.

"Yes. I have millions of aunts and uncles and cousins here. And I don't know any of their names."

"And what, may I ask, is your profession?"

"Oh." She paused. "I teach." Jane reached for the cognac. "At Columbia University."

"A professor?"

"Yes, a professor," replied Jane. "But tell me about your film."

"A professor," Filatov continued undeterred. "A noble profession—teaching the young, seeking the truth."

"But filmmakers, artists—surely they, I mean you, are just as committed. To the truth, I mean."

Filatov appeared not to have heard. "I have a friend," he said, "a painter. His name is Dima. He is a real artist. May I tell you about him?"

Jane took a sip of the cognac and nodded.

"Dima claims to have discovered something called waterness. He says it's a barely perceptible quality of undulation."

"*Waterness?*"

"Yes, that was also my reaction. Water undulates, I said to him. Of course it will have the quality of undulation, or what you call waterness. But Dima believes that all things have this quality. Up in the country, he says he saw a hill with hillness. It was moving, barely, just barely, he said, you could hardly see it, but if you looked, closely and carefully, you'd see that it was undulating. Another time, while traveling by bus along the coast in the Crimea, Dima said he saw that even mountains had mountainness. You mean they were undulating? I said. Yes, that's right, that's it exactly, he said. I told Dima that I see no waterness, regardless of how slowly or deeply I swim. But he said that you can see waterness only when you're not looking for it. You have to look at the water and think of other things, he said, and then, amazingly, the waterness just hits you."

"Was he right?"

"It is a silly story, Miss Jane Sweet, is it not?"

"I think your friend is very perceptive, Mr. Filatov. And so are you."

"He is a true artist. He sees things normal people do not. And"—Filatov moved to let the waitress place the tray on the edge of the table—"I am only half an artist. Unlike Dima, I have no idea what the truth is anymore."

"Where is your friend now?"

"He emigrated to New York," Filatov smiled. "I believe he drives a taxi in Brooklyn."

The waitress shoved the bottles to the side and dropped the plates on the table. Filatov had ordered a lamb shashlik with French fries and parsley. Jane had opted for a plate of pierogis swimming in butter and fried onions.

"Do you visit your family in Lviv often, Miss Jane Sweet?"

"I'm afraid not. I should, I know I should, but there's just never enough time."

"And you live in New York?"

"Yes, on Morningside Heights. Near the university. Have you been to New York, Mr. Filatov?"

"Several times. You will laugh, Miss Jane Sweet, but do you know what I like most about your city? The spaces."

"The parks?"

"No." Filatov paused. "Simple empty spaces. Three, as a matter of fact. The first was next to my hotel, what you Americans call a fleabag. Four green townhouses and an empty lot stood there. The lot was nondescript. It was the space above the four buildings that I loved. It hovered above the houses, Miss Jane Sweet, it exposed the walls of the two corner buildings and the sides of the buildings farther back, and it united the brown of the walls with the green of the buildings and the black of the roofs and the white of the windows in a vibrant whole. They tore down the houses and erected a tall building.

"The second space—that was a few blocks away. It had once been a parking lot, but the cars were gone. Only the little booth with a large sign remained. A chain link fence surrounded the space. Two homeless men lived in shanties built of cardboard boxes, boards, sheet plastic, one or two old mattresses, and some chairs. Whether it rained or snowed, or even if the temperature fell below zero, they stayed. Then, one day, they were gone. The next day, the shacks disappeared as well. Then a hole appeared."

"I understand," Jane nodded. "I feel the same about Vienna."

"My favorite space is still there, Miss Jane Sweet. It is small, squeezed among three tall brown buildings to its left, right, and back. The brick walls are rough, almost jagged. Rows of dirty windows stare down upon the space. Standing on the sidewalk at the edge of the space, your eyes turned upward, you could be in a deep canyon, in a savage mountain range, or perhaps in a medieval castle. I once walked past that space when it was raining heavily. Water poured down the sides of the buildings, flooding the space; the dark sky closed off the top. There I was, alone, with the walls, the water, and the space.

"My most sincere apologies, Miss Jane Sweet, I am rambling about spaces and holes. You must forgive me."

Filatov downed his glass and poured himself another one.

"Artists are unusually sensitive people," he said. "They are like spies. They see things, they hear things, they feel things. But artists cannot be understood. If they could, they would not be artists." Filatov smiled. "You must think I am a sentimental fool."

"I think you're a sad man, Mr. Filatov. And a very sensitive one."

"Whoever said that no man is an island was wrong." Filatov took another pull of vodka. "I am that island."

"It was, I think, John Donne."

"No matter." Filatov waved his hand impatiently. "The point is that man *can* be an island, but that it is impossible to remain in that condition for long."

"I think I understand."

"On the other hand," Filatov smiled, "perhaps it is possible to remain in that condition for long, even forever. Who knows? Perhaps that is life. You know, Miss Jane Sweet, we Russians are by nature a melancholy lot. Always worrying about life, always worrying about death—about God's existence, about God's non-existence, about good, about evil. About everything. And yet, we continue to live and we continue to enjoy life. Perhaps like no other people in the world." Filatov paused, seeming to catch himself. "Excluding, perhaps, only the Ukrainians. But then our two peoples are so alike."

"Americans are no different."

"But you are an exceptional American, Miss Jane Sweet. You have Slavic blood in you. I am not surprised that you understand me." Filatov poured himself a hundred grams. "You were born in America, Miss Jane Sweet? Like your parents?"

"Yes, I was, on Long Island—do you know it? It's not America. It's definitely not America. So was my mother, but—that's a long story. Basically, my parents came to the United States as refugees."

"After the war?"

"Yes, after the war."

"Ah, so they were Ukrainian nationalists."

"Well, actually," Jane stammered, "only my father was. He fought in the underground, I think. I mean, he did. It was a terrible time. I never fully understood just how terrible."

"He killed Communists," Filatov said flatly.

"I suppose he did. He must have."

"And your mother?"

"She'd been in love with a nationalist. Two, actually."

"The end was not, I suspect, happy."

"The first one was a boy named Slavko," Jane spoke haltingly, unsure of how much she should reveal of what she had forgotten. "He stayed—here—while she left. He was in the underground. He died of tuberculosis, but my mother didn't hear about his death until sometime in the fifties. Her name was supposed to have been on his lips when he died. I don't know if that's true, but it would be a fitting end to such a sad story."

"And the other one?"

"Vlodko. My mother loved him passionately. After the war, when the Soviets came, he was hiding in a bunker with three other boys. The KGB—"

"The NKVD."

"Yes, I suppose so. The NKVD surrounded the forest, and they knew that the Soviets had found them, that they would be caught." Jane stopped and drank some cognac. "When the Soviets uncovered the bunker they were all dead.

"It's amazing to me, it's absolutely amazing what these people did and experienced and how much they suffered for something they believed in. I know I couldn't.

"You know," she continued, "I have this cousin. He lives somewhere around here. His name is Petro. He was born in 1945, but he spent the first few weeks of his life on a sealed train bound for Kazakhstan. His father had been in the underground, like his mother, and when the secret police captured them in Lviv, they were placed on a train packed with other prisoners and shipped off. Petro almost died, but his mother saved him by feeding him garlic every day. His father died in exile, but Petro and his brother Stepan and their mother returned home after Khrushchev's amnesty in 1956. There was no place to go, because everyone was afraid of them, afraid to help, afraid even to speak to them. They were politicals," Jane looked at Filatov, "and politicals were trouble. But their mother managed somehow, and Petro learned to play the violin while Stepan—he was the black sheep—dodged the draft, sat in jail for a few months, and then, when he got out, he formed a rock band." Jane stopped, amazed at how many forgotten details she was able to remember. She finished her drink and refilled her glass.

"There's someone else I want to tell you about," she said breathlessly. "My uncle Ivan. He lives in a sooty little town just south of Lviv. His father was a priest. They arrested him in the late forties, and he spent four years in jail. So did Ivan. They placed him in solitary confinement for two years, but he told me that it didn't bother him. He played games, counted bricks, prayed, and whiled away the time, more or less at peace with himself. After they released him, he was blacklisted for many years, but eventually he got a job in a pharmaceuticals factory. He said the best thing about it was that he could steal ten liters of alcohol every week. He was always well stocked at home.

"It's amazing, isn't it?"

"Yet another sad story, Miss Jane Sweet. Why do you come to Lviv when there is so much sadness here?"

"I don't know. I honestly don't know."

"Would it not be easier to forget?"

"That's the strange part," said Jane. "I *had* forgotten. No, that's not quite it. What I mean is, I thought I never knew these things. But obviously I did know them. And now, I can't help remembering them—even though I don't remember ever knowing them."

"We are all prisoners of our culture and upbringing," said Filatov. "We cannot escape them. You tried and failed. I did not and I also failed."

"This time I don't understand."

"Unlike you, Miss Jane Sweet, I embraced my country. Unfortunately—"

"But that's good, isn't it? Why is that failure?"

"Unfortunately, it did not survive my embraces. You see, my country—"

"The Soviet Union?"

"Yes, my country was the Soviet Union. And I am a Soviet man with no home."

"But," Jane said hesitantly, "isn't Russia your home?"

"I am a foreigner there."

"But you speak the language, you live the culture, you eat the food, you wear the clothes."

"Even so, I am a stranger in a strange land."

"But you're Russian. How can you be a stranger to Russia?"

"I feel no love, no passion, no loyalty to it."

Jane looked at him. "You would betray it?"

"You can only betray your own country. Russia is not my country." Filatov waved his hand dismissively. "Imagine, Miss Jane Sweet, if you had to call Long Island your country."

"Good God," she laughed, "I'd die!"

It was the pounding in her head that awoke Jane. The shades were drawn, but a crooked line of light seemed to float in the room. She rubbed her eyes and pressed her fingers against the sides of her head and rubbed the back of her neck. There was alcohol in the air and her hair smelled of cigarette smoke. What a miserable way to begin the day—especially as she had so much to do. But what a fitting way to begin a day in this miserable country. What I need, she thought, is a drink. No wonder this place is so run down. They're always drinking, drunk, or hoping to get drunk. No wonder nothing gets done. They think they have all the time in the world, but they don't. Good God, and neither do I.

As Jane lifted herself from the bed, she turned her head and recognized Fila-tov. What have I done? I have violated every rule in the book. What in God's name have I done? She slipped on her dress, rolled up her underwear, and placed her feet in the pumps. Filatov was breathing heavily. Who is he? Who the hell is that man? She crossed the carpeted room and quietly opened the heavy door. Mercifully, it did not squeak. Minutes later she was in her own room.

How the hell did I wind up in his bed? They had talked and drunk for what seemed like hours. Depending on your perspective, time either stood still or whizzed by. Either way, she vaguely recalled that they had laughed a lot and that at some point in the conversation she had moved her chair closer to his. She also recalled how she had taken his tie in her hand and stroked it. He hadn't drawn back. Instead, he took her hand. In order to prove some point? In order to illus-trate something? And then they had paid. No, it was he who had paid, and they had stumbled out of the restaurant and gone to the elevator—she had said that she couldn't possibly walk up the stairs and he had laughed—and when they were inside—yes, it was just then, when they were inside and the doors had closed and the elevator had begun moving—he somehow managed to press her to his body, and she hadn't resisted, and they kissed. And what happened then? Good God, we fucked and, heaven help me, I may get fucked. Still, it was amazing—the encounter, the conversation, the kiss, the lovemaking. Nothing like this had ever happened in her years with State, nothing quite this amorous that is. There had been a few affairs, but they had been stolid and predictable and boring. This, on the other hand, this was something else. To fuck some strange Russian in an Aus-trian hotel in Ukraine. That was a step up in the world. She was astonished by her own audacity. True, she had been drunk and unaccountable. True, she hadn't quite planned this and she certainly might have acted differently if sober. Still, it was an astounding achievement.

Jane stepped into the bathtub and drew the shower curtain. The lukewarm water sputtered out of the faucet, and as it wet her body she noticed that she smelled, pleasantly, of sweat and sex. She lathered her underarms and crotch, wincing slightly at the soreness of her vagina. How we must have fucked. She remembered mounting him. She remembered his hands searching the crevices of her body, sliding down her breasts, caressing her belly, and plunging into her cunt. Jane shuddered as she ran her fingers along her labia and gently touched her clitoris. I am wet again, I smell of sex again. She lowered herself into the bathtub and, as the water sprinkled her face and ran down her breasts, she spread her legs and slid her hands between them.

Jane brushed her hair carelessly and resisted the temptation to wear the same dress she had on yesterday. I am meeting a slimy professor, she reminded herself, better a solid-looking gray pants suit guaranteed to ward off attention. She decided against having breakfast in the hotel—Anatoly might be in the dining room—and instead took the side stairs to the ground floor and, after scanning the lobby, ran for the exit. It was, as usual, overcast and drizzling. The brightly lit McDonald's was empty. She walked for several blocks. Appropriately enough, the Viennese Cafe was open. After a double espresso and—heaven help me—a small cognac, she felt better and walked outside.

It was true, cognac did help. It did wonders in Lviv and in New York and in Vienna. Everywhere, as a matter of fact. She remembered a Mr. Hladun, some friend of the family, who was supposed to have been an actor or a singer from Argentina. He was also a drunk. She recalled his ringing the doorbell, shouting her father's name, while her mother and the children hid behind the door, quiet, praying that he would go away. Why had Hladun come to New York via Argentina? What had he done during the war? Her best friend in the third and fourth grades probably had a war criminal for a father. I remember him now. He was completely bald, had a dreadful temper, and would beat the kids whenever he had too much to drink. He had served in the Foreign Legion, in Indochina, after the war, and then, in the mid-sixties, one day Tanya announced that her father had changed the family name. Back to the real name, apparently. No one knew why anyone would do that, but now it seemed obvious.

Jane walked, her head uncovered, through the rain. The sky was oppressively gray, but the wet buildings appeared more colorful than when dry. The colors were richer, deeper. The roofs glistened and large puddles collected at every corner. The cobblestones reminded her, absurdly enough, of herds of turtles. Occasionally she had to negotiate her way past phalanxes of black umbrellas, but mostly the sidewalks were empty. As usual, small Soviet-made cars rattled along the streets. She saw a kiosk and decided to buy a newspaper. Maybe I can read this. As the invisible woman handed her the change, Jane asked if she also had beer. Yes, was the answer, but it's warm. Give me a bottle, Jane said, and could you open it, please? The please was unnecessary, she realized, something she'd have to remember. The hand extended the beer bottle and Jane drank from it greedily as she resumed walking. When she finished, she tossed the empty bottle over a fence and listened to it break.

Jane suddenly recalled the ferry ride with baba and her parents. They stood on the deck, watching the buildings glide by. The gulls trailed them; the clouds hid the sun. They pulled alongside the pier and disembarked. She suggested that they walk along the shore, past the abandoned warehouses and dilapidated docks. The sky was gray, and it began to rain just as they reached the jagged end of one of the piers. As they walked back, following the gouges and ruts in the tarmac, wondering how they appeared and when, listening to the waves lap against the rotting poles, she stopped and, turning around, traced her arms along the horizon and said, Can you imagine that ocean liners used to dock here? Her hair and shirt were wet, but she continued to stand in one spot, motionless, her arms stretched out and a smile on her face.

By the time she reached the Polish consulate her hair and clothes were thoroughly wet, but she didn't care. She rang the doorbell next to the massive oak doors. As the door opened, she showed the guard her diplomatic passport and said, "My name is Jane Sweet. Of the American embassy in Vienna. I am here to see Professor Bazarov."

CHAPTER 8

▼

The red-cheeked soldier discreetly closed the door to the richly decorated sitting room. Jane took a step inside and stopped. So this was the elusive son of a bitch. Seated comfortably on an antique chaise longue, the professor was reading a Polish newspaper and sipping a coffee from a porcelain cup. *Why the hell would anyone want to kill* you?

Bazarov looked up and smiled.

"Please join me," he said graciously, "the Poles make excellent coffee. But they are masters at everything, aren't they?" He waved at the chair to his right. "Please, come sit down."

Bazarov took in Jane's appearance.

"No umbrella, I take it. A long journey?"

"Very long," snapped Jane. "Much too long. I am tired and annoyed and bored, professor. Tired by having to chase you. Annoyed by your antics. And bored by your predictability. So let's get to business, professor." Jane walked up to the chaise longue and peered down at Bazarov.

"Who's trying to kill you and why do you want me?"

"Well, when I called Vienna"—Bazarov drew his head back—"I certainly didn't expect them to send a hysterical—"

"I am with the United States Department of State, Mr. Bazarov, so stop bullshitting me and stop wasting my time. Of course," she pointed in the direction of the door, "if you don't need our assistance, I'd be happy to leave you on your own. Vienna is very nice at this time of the year, and I have much work to do."

"Now, now"—Bazarov pushed the chair toward Jane—"please sit down. You are making me nervous. Perhaps you might tell me your name."

Jane observed Bazarov closely. He was a small man, with an insistent face and a bulbous nose, overgrown eyebrows perched above darting eyes, an unkempt mustache, and unusually red lips. His dark hair was combed straight back, creating the impression that his forehead, already broad, was even broader. Thick strands of curly hair protruded from his ears. He wore a neatly pressed three-piece gray suit, white shirt, and red silk tie. His hands were large, and he had flashy rings on two fingers of his right hand. His shoes were black and expensive. The man was obviously a *bon vivant*. And he had taste, or had a tailor with taste. Saving this man from whoever was trying to kill him—if, indeed, someone was—was going to be a thankless job.

"Tell me what happened," she said. "Exactly."

Bazarov leaned back, took out a gold case, and lit a cigarette. He inhaled deeply and let out a smoke ring.

"You don't mind, do you?"

"Just get on with your story, professor."

"Miss Sweet, do you know that I am an émigré from the Soviet Union? And that I was a dissident?"

Jane stared at him in response.

"The KGB tried to kill me then," he said with a note of finality. "They are trying to kill me now."

"Then? When? And how? You never mentioned this in your immigration application."

"In the seventies, Miss Sweet. Many times. I was a refusenik."

"You're not Jewish, professor."

"But my wife—"

"—a woman you married out of convenience—"

"—was. It doesn't matter, Miss Sweet, who was and who was not really Jewish. The point is they treated me as a refusenik. And they tried to kill me."

"How?"

"A car almost hit me. I was beaten up several times. It was terrible."

"But you never mentioned any of this. Why?"

"I was," Bazarov closed his eyes and knit his brow, "escaping from my past, my terrible past. I did not want to be known as a political—and have to get involved with your colleagues across the Potomac. That is something that you, as an American, cannot understand."

"So why try again now? Why not three or two or five years ago? Or just after you came out? Wouldn't that have made more sense, professor?"

"They are settling old scores, I suppose. Perhaps there is a power struggle in the Kremlin? Perhaps the old guard is rearing its head? Or the new guard? Who knows?" Bazarov blew a series of smoke rings in Jane's direction. "Do you? I know I don't."

"And your three friends? Also a settling of old scores?"

"A diversion," said Bazarov tersely. "I am sure they are after me. The others were merely in the way."

"But that's what I still don't understand. Why would the KGB have scores to settle with an American university professor? Maybe you were a dissident twenty or thirty years ago. And maybe they beat you up a couple of times. But you sure as hell weren't a Solzhenitsyn—and Solzhenitsyn seems to be doing quite well in Russia, professor—and you sure as hell aren't very interesting or important anymore." Jane watched to see how he would react to this barb. "Or are you?"

"I am an intellectual," Bazarov replied. "It is my obligation to tell the truth."

"And what sort of truth do you tell? I mean, what sort of truth would be worth killing you over?"

"Ask them."

"I would, professor, I gladly would, but since I don't know who they are, I can't. You see my problem, don't you?" Jane pointed to the coffee pot. "I'll have that coffee after all."

"When I escaped, Miss Sweet, I chose truth. Viktor Kravchenko chose freedom, but I chose truth. Can you understand that? My life, my whole life, has been a repudiation of their lies." He uncrossed his legs as if to emphasize the point and poured Jane a cup. "The *kawka*, Miss Sweet, is poetry."

"Tell me, professor," Jane said, as she sipped the coffee, "tell me something about your work for the Mir Foundation."

"I was fortunate to win a most generous grant," he replied. Oh, how cool you are, Jane thought, you haven't even batted an eyelid. "For a worthy cause—building civil society in eastern Europe."

"But tell me, professor," Jane recalled Bristol's caustic remarks, "tell me just how one goes about building civil society. I never could understand what that means."

"I will try to make it simple—"

"Please do, professor."

"—since you are not an expert." Bazarov made a sweeping gesture with the two fingers holding the cigarette. "Civil society consists of autonomous public institutions. Churches, clubs, parties—"

"And you are going to found churches, Professor Bazarov?"

"—social movements, trade unions, and so on." Bazarov paused. "I have no intention of founding churches, Miss Sweet. I am not a priest. I only live for the truth."

"So how did you and your three dead friends hope to build this civil society? By telling the truth?"

"By building capacity. By providing the local populations of these countries with the skills to build their own institutions."

"That's something else I could never understand, professor. I could never understand how you go about building an institution. With bricks and cement, or what?"

"Not quite, Miss Sweet. With knowledge. With skills."

"But what are the skills one needs to build—oh, say, a church? And these skills, whatever they are—I assume you and your friends had them?"

"We are not priests, Miss Sweet, but we provided access to people who have the skills to build, if you like, churches. We are the middlemen, Miss Sweet, between buyers and sellers. Except of course that there was no buying and selling. I can assure you that everything was done for altruistic reasons."

"Of course. So tell me, professor, how did you bring these buyers and sellers together? Conferences? Workshops?"

"Precisely. Conferences. Workshops."

"In the West?"

"Where else? In Siberia? In Vienna, as a matter of fact."

"And whom did you invite? To these conferences and workshops in Vienna, I mean."

"Activists. Local activists. People who want a better life for themselves and their children." Bazarov pointed at Jane with the cigarette. "This is not America, Miss Sweet. Rugged individualism is not second nature."

"So these people, these men—and women?—applied for these conferences— they filled out application forms, right?—and, after you chose them, they would come to Vienna, learn skills, and go back home to build civil society. Is that right, professor? That's all there was to it, right?"

"*Exactement.*"

"So why would anyone want to kill you for this? I don't understand. Those were professional hits—"

Bazarov looked at Jane quizzically.

"—assassinations. That points to either the KGB—heavens knows they have enough underemployed assassins—or the mafiya. But the secret police stopped killing professors in the fifties and the mafiya only kills policemen and other criminals."

Jane looked at Bazarov. He sat impassively on the chaise longue. God, she thought, I am more nervous than he is. This is child's play for him.

"Which means," she continued, "that if it wasn't the KGB and if you aren't politicians, then you must be crooks and your killer must be the mafiya. Q.E.D."

"I admire your logic, but it is fuzzy." He smiled. "As, alas, with all women. You see, Miss Sweet, we are not the victims of the secret police as an institution, as in Stalin's times, but, I fear, of rogue agents, out to pay us back for what we did to them in the past."

"But, as far as I can tell, you did nothing to them in the past—certainly nothing worth killing you for today. I don't think you're being entirely honest with me, professor." Jane rose from her seat.

"Now listen, professor. Let me tell you what I think. First, your project with the Mir Foundation is nothing more than some kind of money-laundering scheme. Second, you stole the money. And third, whoever your partners are in Russia decided to punish you for that theft. You are not a dissident, you have probably never been a dissident. And you are far too mediocre to merit killing." Jane looked down at Bazarov with what she hoped were piercing eyes. "But you are one stupid son of a bitch to believe you could hoodwink the Russian mafiya."

Bazarov let out a deep breath and extended both hands, palms outward.

"You have caught us," he said. "I have underestimated your powers of detection, Miss Sweet, and for this I apologize." He clasped his hands. "Except for one minor detail. I was not the thief. I would never steal money. *Jamais.* Nor would my colleagues, Clausen and Sosenko. It was Kanapa. He was the embezzler, but when we found out, it was too late." He rested his hands in his lap. "That is the truth, the whole truth, and nothing but the truth."

You fucking liar, thought Jane, you motherfucking liar. You're passing the buck because they're dead. Why did you run? Why didn't you just come to us immediately, in Vienna? Why didn't you report this right away? You fucking liar. It was time to wrap this up.

"By the way, professor, what's your connection with the Women's Institute in Kiev?"

"They provided us with trainees," replied Bazarov, "women trainees."

"For the conferences?"

"Of course."

"I understand there are women's institutes in other cities. Tel Aviv, Berlin—"

"Istanbul and New York. Wherever there are large concentrations of émigrés."

"And women."

"Women are émigrés too, Miss Sweet."

"But that's not all they are, professor, is it? By the way, professor, I hear that Brighton Beach has some terrific nightclubs."

"I imagine so. Russians know how to enjoy life."

"And your trainees, professor. Did they enjoy life?"

"Of course, Miss Sweet. Empowerment can only enhance a woman's life."

Jane could not resist a smile.

"Let's talk about these trainees, who came to the West to be empowered, professor. They came for a few days or a few weeks, and then went home?"

"Yes, they came for the conferences and then went home."

"Were any from Lviv?"

"I should think so. Of course."

"Would you know their names?"

"Alas, no. But here's our last conference program. All the names are there. And their affiliations." Bazarov rummaged in his briefcase and handed Jane a small brochure. "Be my guest."

The conference had taken place several months ago in Vienna, in some small hotel in the third district, where the east Europeans congregate. The program seemed genuine enough, but the list of participants included only Bazarov, Kanapa, Sosenko, and Clausen—and some twenty to thirty women from Kiev, Lviv, Odessa, Kharkiv, and a number of places Jane did not recognize.

"Where are the experts? The trainers?"

"Local Viennese, sometimes Poles and Hungarians," Bazarov replied. "They always change, so we never put their names in the brochures."

"I want to speak to"—Jane randomly chose one of the names—"this woman. Oksana Matvienko." She rose and went to the door. "You wait here."

The program identified Matvienko as a teacher at a local trade school.

"Where is it located?" Jane asked one of the consular officials, a short man with a pince nez, a bow tie, and a pencil-thin mustache.

"In side street near cemetery," he answered.

"Can you show me on the map?"

"You should visit graves of Polish heroes of war of independence," he suggested. "They were destroyed, but Polish state recently rebuilt them. Who knows how long they last." After a pause he added, "Here." He extended his long fore-finger and pressed it to the map. "See? Exactly here."

"Yes," replied Jane, "exactly here. Thank you." The official bowed slightly and planted a loud kiss on her hand.

"*Do widzenia, pani,*" he said.

"Good-bye," Jane replied. But you weren't supposed to touch my hand with your lips. Don't you know that?

The rain had stopped, but the cloud cover remained, a thick layer of wet cotton suspended above the sodden buildings. There is no sun here, Jane thought. How can these people live without sun? No wonder they are so morose. No wonder everything is falling apart—the streets, the sidewalks, the walls, the stoops, the doors, the balconies. And the country. Why repair anything when the sky could cave in on you any second?

As Jane passed a pizzeria, she heard footsteps behind her. Involuntarily, she hastened her pace.

"Miss Jane Sweet!" a familiar voice called out. She turned and saw Filatov, carrying an umbrella and wearing a long trenchcoat.

"What a coincidence," he said. "I am so happy to have run into you. This morning, when I woke up, I had thought—"

"I was in a hurry. Sorry." She smiled hesitantly. "It was a lovely evening."

"Yes, it was. May I accompany you? You are going to see a long lost relative?"

"No," she said, thinking of what to say. "A school teacher, a friend of a friend. It would bore you."

"Not at all."

"You are a curious man, Anatoly. Suicidal one day, devil may care the next. I wonder what your game is."

"I have no game, Miss Jane Sweet. I am only killing time."

The school was situated in a charcoal-gray building sandwiched between a working-class bar and a muddy bus depot. The facade was covered with dark blotches indicating the absence of plaster. A washed out blue and yellow flag drooped above the entrance, which led into a dank corridor paved with stained floorboards and flanked by decaying green walls. Just before the wooden staircase on the right was a door with a sign in almost illegible Cyrillic. Jane couldn't make out the writing.

"The director's office," said Filatov. "Just knock loudly and walk in."

The room they entered was painted a light green; its high ceiling was white. A worn-out runner extended diagonally from the entrance to a door on the left. A middle-aged woman in a beige blouse sat behind a light wooden desk. Next to it stood two chairs and a leafy plant in a brightly colored ceramic pot. Several portraits of mustachioed men in embroidered shirts and fur hats adorned the walls. The woman looked up from her newspaper as Jane and Filatov walked in. Jane cleared her throat, but Filatov spoke first.

"Excuse us," he said in Russian, "but we would like to speak to the director."

"*A kto Vy?*" the woman replied, also in Russian.

"This is Professor Jane Sweet, of Columbia University. My name is Anatoly Sergeevich Filatov. I am a filmmaker from Moscow. We are working on a project on education in Ukraine."

"One moment, please," the woman answered, "I will speak to the director. Please wait." She pointed at the chairs.

"What did you tell her?" Jane asked as soon as the door to the director's office closed. "My Russian is rusty."

"That we are working on a project. On Ukrainian education."

"But why didn't you just ask for Matvienko?"

"One cannot be direct with these people. They will always suspect you of having ulterior motives. This way, we give them the motives and they take us seriously."

The door opened and the woman motioned them inside. Although larger and adorned with more plants and portraits, the room was an exact replica of the secretary's. A white-haired man in faded brown corduroy pants and a light blue short-sleeved shirt rose to greet them. His hair was parted in the middle and his thick glasses had bulky black frames. The ashtray on his desk was overflowing with cigarette butts. Jane coughed as she entered. Filatov took a cigar out of his breast pocket and stuck it in his mouth.

"Welcome, welcome," the director said in Ukrainian, "welcome to the Ivan Franko Trade School. Please sit down."

To Jane's surprise, Filatov answered in equally fluent Ukrainian.

"We are honored," he said, bowing slightly. Where did he learn these west Ukrainian mannerisms?

"I would," said Jane in her hesitant Ukrainian, "I mean, *we* would like to see Mrs. Oksana Matvienko. She is one of your teachers, I believe, and—"

"—and we are," continued Filatov, "delighted that you can spare us some of your precious time. Perhaps a cigar?" He extended a packet toward the director. "They are Cuban. Perhaps your colleagues would like some too.

"You see," said Filatov after the director pocketed the cigars, "we are profiling school directors"—he waved his right hand at the man—"in order to show how independent Ukraine is building its own educational institutions." Jane almost winced at his choice of words. "I understand," he added confidentially, "how difficult it must be, after centuries of Russification."

As the director opened his mouth to speak, Filatov quickly added, "We will of course reimburse you for your time."

"Oh, no, that's quite unnece—"

"Of course it isn't," Filatov gently brushed aside his objection. "You are a busy man. We understand. And then," he paused, "if we could also speak to Mrs. Matvienko? About day-to-day teaching, her personal experiences, her woman's perspective."

"Oh, but that won't be possible."

"But why?" asked Jane. "We won't take much of her time."

"She is in Europe."

"At a conference on civil society?"

"Ah," said the director, "she went to some conference several months ago. In Vienna. She hasn't returned. You know"—now it was his turn to adopt a confidential tone—"there are too many of these conferences. Our young people will do anything to stay in the West."

"Do you know where she is?" Jane asked. "Is she still in Vienna?"

"Nina! Nina Andriivna!" cried the director. The woman who guarded the anteroom rushed in and stood, almost apologetically, before his desk.

"Do you know where Oksana Fedorivna is? She sends you postcards, doesn't she?"

"Why yes," replied the woman. "Yes, she's somewhere in Italy. I have postcards from Rome, from Milan. Mostly from Milan."

"*Konferentsii?*" Jane inquired.

"Oh, no, Oksana Fedorivna is working. Making pizza. These are hard times in independent Ukraine. People do what they can."

"But life will get better after we have a new president," said the director. "God help us, life will get better." Jane nodded, while Filatov tapped his cigar on the ashtray.

"But let me tell you about the Ivan Franko Trade School," he said with visible pride. "We are innovators. We are the future. We are the next generation."

When they finally emerged from the building, Jane turned to Filatov. "You're not just an artist, Anatoly, you're a con artist. I'm impressed."

"Do not be. I know these people. We have the same mentality. Even if I am Russian and they are Ukrainian. We are, you know, all Soviet.

"You understand, of course," he added, "that your friend is a prostitute."

Yes, Anatoly, I've known since Kiev.

They parted near the Opera. A large crowd was listening to some woman denounce the Kremlin for interfering in Ukraine's elections. The people cheered. The ubiquitous orange stood out against their dark coats. An earnest young man with a handlebar mustache approached Jane and pinned a small orange ribbon to her lapel. American diplomats shouldn't be taking sides, she thought, should they? The crowd broke into chants of "*za vil'nu Ukrainu.*" But if they want a free Ukraine, why not? She decided to leave the pin on.

Jane hailed a taxi and headed back to the Polish consulate. A wave of deep exhaustion swept through her body, as she sat slumped in the back seat. The rocking of the car, the smell of the cigarettes, the dampness of her clothes—all intensified the nausea she had begun feeling in the school. Everything here is rotten, she thought. Everything around me is decayed. The place smelled of death, that's what it was. Death was all around—in the grimy gutters, the dark hallways, the overgrown cemeteries, the peeling facades, the wooden floors, the dusty plants, the corduroy trousers, the thick-soled shoes, the henna-colored hair, the purple mascara. The sky *should* fall on this place. Perhaps the clouds would smother everything and everybody, and then, when it was over, life—normal life, life without the wars and the trains and the concentration camps—could resume. Perhaps then this wretched country could, as that crowd hoped, be free. Or at least be free to forget its past.

Good God, it dawned on her, I am talking just like baba! I am thinking just like baba! A broad smile appeared on Jane's face. See, baba? After all these years, you have finally made me laugh.

Hey, baba, can you see me? I can see *you*—sitting in the backyard, of course, going on and on about something that only now makes sense. And there you are, too, mama, knitting as usual. And tato—what else?—is drinking a beer, straight from the can. And I am playing with dolls, trying not to listen, pretending not to listen, listening. And when the sun sets and the day comes to an end, you talk about the only thing you always talk about—the war. *Which war? I used to wonder. I know now which war.* When the Soviets came in 1939, someone says, it could be baba—*but it could also be me*—they came as liberators, but soon they showed their true face. The soldiers were the worst, but the officers, dressed in those ridiculous uniforms lined with rows of medals, were little better. Their stupid wives thought that nightgowns were evening dresses. They never realized that they were strolling along the boulevards in pajamas. Then they began arresting people. The first were the nationalists. Then it was the intellectuals and priests. People began speaking Russian in public, going to communist rallies, joining the Party. And then came June, and the Soviets turned into animals. First they filled the cellars, then they killed the prisoners, then they set fire to the prisons. When the Germans arrived, wearing their neat uniforms, marching in step, with looks of determination on their handsome faces, everyone was relieved. Remember that? Yes, I remember, someone says. *And I remember.*

It is mama's turn. *Go ahead, mama, tell me your story.* After the Germans came, fires broke out throughout the city. The prisons were opened and the stench of dead flesh was all around us. Bodies covered the red grass, laid out like rotting fish. Women went from corpse to corpse, holding wet handkerchiefs to their faces, their eyes red, their lips quivering. The bodies had no faces, only heads; some had no arms, no legs, only torsos. Some torsos had no stomachs. Bits of flesh lay strewn about, bits of rags covered the rotting corpses, shoes poked out from beneath mounds of flesh, a thick smell filled the air, as the women went from flesh to flesh, looking for signs of recognizable body parts or clothes. Volodymyr was placed into a pine coffin a few centimeters too short for him. The lid was kept on during the service. The entire family wept. They carried the body to the cemetery down the road, with Irena weeping hysterically and Slava trying to comfort her. Squadrons of warplanes flew overhead.

Jane's eyes filled with tears. *See? I weep with you.*

Baba starts again. The Communists had escaped, so they beat the Jews. Remember that? *Oh, yes.* The police rounded up the Jews. Leave your belongings at home, they said. The Jews were collected in the main square and told to march down the road, toward the forest. Their faces were expressionless, their eyes resigned. The people peeked out from behind their curtains. Where were they taking them? Why don't they run? Why don't they run? One hour later volleys of gunfire came from the hills, and the people shook their heads and were ashamed to look into one another's eyes. Remember that? *Yes, I do.*

Tanks stood at the intersections. The Germans seized the post office, telegraph, and other communications points. A blue and yellow flag adorned the cultural society building on the main square. Boys with armbands patrolled the streets; black-uniformed men in shiny leather boots and black caps strutted along the boulevard. From the distance artillery fire punctuated the nervous stillness.

The corpses were left on the streets. Silent figures crept up in the dark and tugged them down side streets. Remember that? *Yes, I remember that, too.*

When the bombs began falling, mama says, we hid under the table. We crouched there, shivering, too scared to listen, too scared not to listen. Once, a bomb fell into our yard, maybe twenty meters from the house. It made a terrifying sound, we were sure we would die, but it only left a huge crater where the outhouse had once stood. My uncle laughed when he saw where it had fallen. Just like the Russians, he said. *See? I'm also laughing!*

I said—baba is speaking—good-bye with tears streaming down my face. They embraced me tightly; everyone cried. Cannon fire could be heard in the east; the *Bolsheviki* were coming. It was time to go. We squeezed into the train going west. The station was packed. Come with us, children said. No, we will manage, their parents answered. The train began pulling out of the station. Handkerchiefs waved, tears flowed. The town grew smaller until it disappeared behind the hills. *I remember that, too, baba.*

Tato says nothing. He sits drinking beer and squinting at the setting sun. *You have fought Communists. You have killed Russians. What can you say?*

"*My tut,*" announced the cab driver. "We're here."

Jane looked around her, surprised that she could no longer hear the bombs and screams.

"*Poe-lahnd con-sue-late,*" he said.

Jane almost stumbled on the curb. What am I doing here? she thought, as she collected the papers that fell from her bag. Why am I helping a man who deserves to be marched to the forest and shot?

How was she to live with the creeping realization that Bazarov was even more despicable than she could possibly have imagined? A slimy bastard, a dishonest son of a bitch, a thief, a money-launderer, a traitor to his friends—and now, also a pimp. Whoever was trying to kill him had at least a million good reasons to kill him. And the worst thing was that Bazarov was hoping—no, he was obviously *expecting*—to get away with it.

She found Bazarov in the library, a large room lined with bookshelves extending from the ceiling to the floor. He was seated at a desk, dressed impeccably, and thumbing through some thin volume.

"*Will the Non-Russians Rebel?*" he said, his eyebrows raised.

"I have no idea, professor, but the people outside just might."

"It's a book." He showed her the red cover. "How strange. This is the copy I left on the airplane."

"Oksana Matvienko is a prostitute," Jane said flatly.

Bazarov looked up at her with a look of puzzlement. Jane stared back.

"How tragic," he finally said, shaking his head. "How terribly tragic."

"And you know nothing about it?"

"Miss Sweet, how could I possibly know anything about it? I am an intellectual and, even if you do not believe me, that is all I am."

"How do you suppose she became a prostitute, professor?"

"How should I know? How could I possibly divine her subjectivity?"

"Oh, fuck your subjectivity," Jane said impatiently. "Let's just see if we can make sense of this. First, she applies to take part in your conference in Vienna. Then she arrives and actually takes part. While there, she learns all sorts of skills for building—how did you put it, professor?—the institutions of civil society. But instead of returning home and applying these skills, she decides, 'What the hell. Why not go to Italy and walk the streets?' Is that about right, professor?

"Some program you got there, professor, some"—Jane hesitated, choosing her words carefully—"fucking program you got there."

"We all make mistakes, Miss Sweet. I am sure you have also made mistakes."

"So Matvienko was just a bad apple, is that right? Escaped your eagle eyes? Could happen to anyone, professor, right?"

"Exactly, my dear Miss Sweet. That is exactly what must have happened. She fell through the cracks."

"You mean she was *pushed* through the cracks."

"If you say so, Miss Sweet."

It was no use continuing this conversation. At least not here, where he feels safe and I have no leverage. She would take him back to Vienna, perhaps even to the United States, and the investigation could be resumed there. And since he'd be dependent on the government to hide him, they'd be able to work on him at their own pace.

"Miss Sweet," said Bazarov, "may I make a small suggestion? Try not to curse. Foul language does not become a woman. Especially one wearing an orange ribbon. Have you joined the masses, Miss Sweet?"

"I'll take that under fucking advisement," she replied and walked out of the library. "We leave tomorrow at noon," she called back. "By train."

What were you saying, baba? Finish your story. As the train leaves the station, we peer out the windows. Gentle yellow hills and large white clouds surround us. Some of the women are waving. The men in shabby hats are smoking. I crane my neck out the window and wave back. *You will never return. Did you ever suspect that? But look, baba, I'm here.* Thick, black smoke rises from beyond the hills, where the *Bolsheviki* are advancing. They are burning villages, destroying churches, arresting everyone again. What could we do but flee? We couldn't stay. That would have meant certain death. We had no choice. So we ran. We boarded the train and hoped to escape the killing. We were innocent. We just wanted to live. *But not everyone is innocent, baba. I know. Some people don't deserve to live, baba. I know that, too.*

Filatov was waiting for her in the hotel lobby, a rose in his hand. "*Küss die Hand, gnädige Frau,*" he said in his best Viennese manner. She extended her hand and he raised it to his lips. Will he, like the Pole who should have known better, actually kiss it? He won't, of course he won't. When he did not, Jane could not repress a knowing smile. Anatoly could be from Vienna or—the thought almost made her laugh—Lviv.

Filatov took Jane by the arm and escorted her into the restaurant. He had already reserved a table. On it stood a bottle each of vodka, cognac, and champagne, and two bottles of beer, Fanta, and mineral water—testimony, she smiled again, to the man's contradictory nature, in this case his residual Soviet habit of ordering as much as possible immediately, before the restaurant ran out of supplies. Filatov guided her to the table and, as the night before, pulled out the chair for her to sit on.

"This is too much, Anatoly. You are a crazy Russian."

"Alas no. I am just Russian. All Russians are crazy."

Jane was silent throughout most of the meal.

"Today, *you* are despondent, Miss Jane Sweet."

"Not despondent, Anatoly. Confused."

Filatov filled their glasses with cognac.

"There is," Jane continued, "too much dead history here. I feel it in the streets. The buildings—they press in on me. Those crooked windows, those broken window panes, those damned cobblestones, those gables and spires—it's all too much."

"I know," he said, "I know exactly what you mean. The dead are watching us, they are constantly following us."

"I should feel depressed, but I don't. That's the strange thing, Anatoly. That's what I don't understand. The dead are all around us. They're hiding in shadows, lurking in alleys, sitting in cafes, driving buses. I should be terrified, and in a way I am. I should want to get out of here as quickly as possible. And I do. And yet I don't. Good God, Anatoly, I'm even wearing one of those orange pins!"

"It doesn't matter what you wear. The dead are waiting." Filatov raised his glass, as if in a toast. "For us, of course."

"How ghoulish we've become. Is this what they mean by the melancholy Slavic soul?"

"But don't you see, Ivanka?" Jane was shocked to hear him use her Ukrainian name. "Don't you see"—he had noticed the stunned look on her face—"that you have become one of us?"

They parted next morning in the lobby of the hotel. Filatov was waiting for her as she came down the marble staircase. He was holding a large bouquet of red carnations.

"You are an incurable romantic, Anatoly."

"A *Soviet* romantic."

"I must go," she whispered, "they are waiting for me in Vienna."

He nodded.

"*Küss die Hand, gnädige Frau.*"

"Will you still be here tomorrow?"

"I have some work to do before I go back to Moscow. Call me at the hotel."

"You better be in. Or," she added, almost as an afterthought, "I'll pump ya full of lead."

CHAPTER 9

▼

They boarded the Moscow-Vienna train just before noon. The olive-green cars were clearly of Soviet vintage. The hammer and sickle had been sloppily painted over, replaced by the Russian two-headed eagle on some cars and the Ukrainian trident on others. The first-class sleeper consisted of eight compartments, and a scrawny red rug snaked down the length of the aisle. Despite the lack of ventilation, the windows were locked shut. Bazarov placed his briefcase in a middle compartment, Jane placed her baggage in the adjacent one. As he sat back and lit a cigarette, she walked down the aisle. One compartment was occupied by the conductor: the bed was unmade, and an empty bottle of beer, a half-eaten apple, and a piece of black bread stood on the slide-out table. All the others were empty—reserved and paid for by the United States Embassy in Kiev. Jane opened the doors to all of them and looked inside. Now I am the Soviet border guard poking around and looking for imperialist propaganda. She asked the conductor to lock all the doors. She checked the gun in her purse. They should be safe. And once they reached the Hungarian border, in about five hours, a car would be waiting for them. Bristol had arranged for a group of CIA people, some from the Budapest embassy, a few others from the Bratislava office, to meet her and take Bazarov back to Vienna. In principle, everything should work. She remembered the old Soviet joke about some yokel who arrives in Moscow and asks for a fabulous department store he'd heard about called Principle. Where'd you hear about it? someone finally asks him. They told me that in Moscow you can get everything in principle, is the answer. Almost imperceptibly, the train began moving, leaving the vaulted Habsburg-era train station behind. How odd, Jane thought. I am actually sad to be leaving this awful place.

She watched the decaying houses pick up speed. Her visit had been completely unplanned. The story had written itself. Had it not been for those three killings and that idiot of an ambassador, I would not be here. Quite possibly, I would never have come here again. But here I am—in a train, in the field, a gun in my purse, a lover at the hotel, an orange ribbon on my coat. Jane waved good-bye to the men in the shabby black hats, the women in the colored kerchiefs, and the prisoners and soldiers heading east. I have fled from the malls of my childhood, I have traveled, I have tried to escape baba's memories, mama's, tato's. And where am I now? I have come full circle. Their memories are not mine, but I have memories of their memories. Does that make this place my home? Am I really absolutely one of them? Who knows where my home is, and who cares? Who the fuck cares? Who the fuck cares what I am? Who the fuck cares who I am? Who the fuck cares where I was born? Who the fuck cares where I belong? The past has freed me of the past. I can do anything I want—without looking forward, without looking backward. Fuck it all. I am *absolyutno* free.

Filatov watched the departing train from behind the newspaper kiosk at the end of the platform. The country was independent, but the kiosks still looked exactly as they had in Soviet times. The sides plastered with magazines and trinkets and postcards, the newspapers neatly arrayed inside, where you couldn't possibly see the titles or the dates, a small window positioned just below a small man's chin, the hands—all you could see were the old hands—that handed you a newspaper, usually folded in two, in exchange for your money. There was one difference. You could now buy pornography and accurate maps.

A car was waiting for him in the parking lot to the left of the station. A black Volga, the kind favored by politicians. Oligarchs drove western cars. He opened the door to the back and climbed in.

"How good to see you, Anatoly Sergeevich."

"The pleasure, Taras Grigorovich, is all mine," replied Filatov.

Colonel Shevchenko offered him a Belomorkanal cigarette.

"So, tell me, Anatoly Sergeevich, how do you intend to proceed?"

"My plan—*our* plan, if you approve—is simple. At Chop, while the train cars are sealed and the carriage is being replaced, I shall shoot him."

"And what about the girl?"

"I shall also shoot her."

"That could be complicated. She's a diplomat. The Americans will protest."

"I know. But you will say that the Russian mafiya was responsible, that the killer escaped." Filatov took a deep drag. Belomorkanals were the cheapest Soviet brand, but he had always savored them. "Of course, you will do everything you can to help. You will even involve your esteemed colleague from the Russian security service." Filatov let out the thick smoke. "And I shall also do everything to help. We shall be outraged, absolutely outraged. But wait, what's this? We shall provide them with documentation on the Italians. White slavery! International crime rings! Prostitution! The headlines will be stupendous. The Germans will be in anguish. The Israelis will protest. The Turks will feign ignorance. The American State Department will issue declarations. The European Union will wring its hands. But you, my dear Taras Grigorovich, you will be a hero—a bold fighter in the global struggle against the evil exploitation of women. Who knows? You might even become ambassador to the United Nations."

"As always, Anatoly Sergeevich, you exaggerate. It's too bad about Miss Sweet. As to Bazarov—"

"I know he defected. And I know you were his case officer."

"*Da*," sighed Shevchenko, "they gave me hell. My career almost ended. By the way, does Jane Sweet know that her escort was once a highly prized asset of her employer?"

"Probably not."

"And does she know about *you?*"

"She hasn't a clue."

"The irony is almost unbearable, don't you think? What strange times we live in."

The Volga hurtled along the poorly paved roads, scattering chickens and geese and occasional cows in its wake. The countryside was hilly and the hills were mostly forested. Suntanned men and women, the men in dusty hats, the women in scarves, knit bags or pails of fruit in their hands, walked along the unpaved side streets. The boys wore shapeless pants, the girls flower-print dresses. Filatov noticed that here too the formerly ubiquitous bows—the large white bows that all Soviet leaders loved—had disappeared. In the distance he could see the foothills of the Carpathians.

This is where his father had fought the nationalists. This is where they had burrowed bunkers and tunnels and hid out, lying in wait to ambush collective farm chairmen, Party workers, Komsomol leaders, and NKVD soldiers. For all he knew, this is where Jane's father may have killed Communists. It took almost ten years to destroy them. The nationalists fought well. They had nothing to lose, so they fought to the death. We lost many good comrades in those years. We felt their absence later, when the era of stagnation swallowed us all.

"My father was killed in Lvov," he remarked, "assassinated by nationalists. Did you know that?"

"Yes," replied Shevchenko. "Those were terrible times."

"I was there when they killed him."

"No child should see the death of his father."

"My mother was also killed."

"They died for a good cause."

"Did they?"

"They died for what they believed in, Anatoly Sergeevich. How many of us can say that today?"

Filatov fell silent again, as Shevchenko lit another cigarette. Was it really necessary for Jane Sweet to be killed? His KGB instincts told him that the answer had to be yes. She was too big of a loose end, and no job, however small, should have loose ends. And yet, what a shame it would be. Do I love her? Filatov asked himself. The answer—*no*—came easily, and he knew that he was not deluding himself, trying to engage in a rationalization that would make the job of execution easier. It wasn't love that caused him to shrink back from the thought of Jane's dying. No, it was the awareness that she shouldn't even be in the line of fire—she didn't deserve to die because she shouldn't be a loose end in a wet job. Ivanka Svit—An agent of imperialism! A representative of monopoly capitalism! An imperialist stooge, a capitalist-roader, a traitor to the proletariat, a defender of the bourgeoisie, a vicious supporter of nationalist crimes against humanity! All the beloved epithets of Communist propaganda flooded Filatov's mind. He recalled the images of the imperialist enemies on Soviet posters—the top hats, the large bellies, the big cigars, the hooked noses, the greedy eyes, the fat lips, the sharp teeth. Jane was the polar opposite of those caricatures. How disappointed his comrades in the old KGB would have been to learn that they had lost the momentous struggle of two—how did our propaganda put it?—incompatible world systems to a confused, fragile, and exceedingly vulnerable woman? Did she really have to be killed? What would the fictional whiskey priest have done in such a case? Alcohol was his means of coping with the demands of a vocation for which he was no match. And yet, despite all his lapses and despite all his transgressions, in the end the priest, when faced with the choice of turning his back on his vocation or sacrificing his life, chose the latter. Whiskey was a solution only when the choice was not momentous, not definitive, when it did not represent the affirmation or repudiation of everything he stood for. Looked at from this perspective, his own dilemma appeared less anguished. Were this a question of his vocation—were he still fighting for communism, however tarnished its vision—then the answer would be obvious. The choice would be to affirm his calling or to reject it. There could be no question about the necessity and inevitability of Jane's death. Her dying would still be tragic, but it would be part of the larger burden—the cross!—that he, as a believer, had to carry. But now—now things were different. Bazarov was a contract killing. Jane's death was ancillary to Bazarov's. True, I admire the mafiya for its sense of honor and faith, but their struggle—and certainly their cause—is not mine. There is no imperative that Jane be killed. I could kill her anyway, that would certainly be cleaner and easier, but I do not *have* to do so. As a whiskey priest, I have the right and the choice to do otherwise. And I choose that she live.

Jane knocked on Bazarov's door. He opened the latch and she walked in. The air was thick with smoke. Bazarov had been reading. Jane noticed that it was something in French.

"You smoke too much," she said.

"It helps me concentrate when I read, Miss Sweet. Unfortunately, I read a lot."

"A novel?"

"Philosophy."

"Really? What is it about?"

"The nature of truth, the duty of intellectuals, the—"

"And what is the duty of intellectuals, professor?"

"To tell the truth to power, of course. To tell it fearlessly. And to live it."

"Always?"

"*Toujours.* There can be no compromise."

"And you—as an intellectual—you always tell the truth and you always live the truth?"

"I try to, but it is always a struggle. Man is imperfect, Miss Sweet."

"And so is woman, professor," Jane said. "Tell me, professor, is it only intellectuals who have the duty to tell the truth—always, that is? What about diplomats like me? Do we have the same duty?"

"Yes, but—"

"But what?"

"—there *is* a difference," continued Bazarov. "Normal people, people who are not intellectuals, should try to tell the truth, but they are rarely in its possession. Intellectuals, on the other hand, *can* possess the truth. And then they must do their duty. It is an imperative, Miss Sweet, not a preference or an exhortation. That is the difference, and it is a big difference."

"Well, yes, professor, but here's something I've never been able to understand. How do intellectuals like yourself *know* they're in possession of the truth? I mean, it can't be that obvious. If it were, then even the *hoi polloi* like me would be able to figure it out."

"One just knows, Miss Sweet."

"And if someone, say another intellectual, disagrees with you? I mean, you guys are always disagreeing about everything, aren't you?"

"Then one of us is wrong and one of us is right. But because we know that, both of us have a duty to affirm the rightness of our views."

"And who's to judge, professor? Who's the umpire?"

"That is obvious, Miss Sweet—the community of intellectuals."

"And the rest of us, what are we supposed to do?"

"That, too, is obvious, Miss Sweet—follow our lead."

"I guess it's just as well, then, that I don't read French. Right, professor?"

Jane took a cigarette from the gold case on the seat. The train had slowed to a crawl. They were in the middle of a lush field, a copse of trees to the right, tall grasses to the left, and a small pond in the middle. A boy in an oversized cap stood on the bank, his bicycle to his side, with a fishing rod in his hands. On the other side of the pond several cows were chewing lazily and swinging their tails. In the distance was a village—generic rooftops and the onion-shaped dome of a church. Behind the village were brown hills.

"You know, professor, I once took a philosophy course."

"Bravissima, Miss Sweet."

"I don't remember much, but I remember writing a paper about truth."

"A complicated notion," Bazarov said. "'I never speak the truth.' The liar's paradox."

"My paper was more prosaic. I wrote that there are four kinds of truth-lie combinations. There are truths and there are lies. But there are also half-truths and half-lies. Truth telling may be preferable to lying, but both require courage. Telling the truth and telling a lie also presuppose knowing what you want. In that sense, truth telling is like lying; it's a kind of anti-lying."

"Very clever, Miss Sweet."

"Yeah, but you know what really intrigued me? Half-truths and half-lies. I said they were in the no-man's land between truth and falsehood. I also said that both presupposed cowardice and that both rested on lack of will. You'd think they were identical, except that half-truths are acts of hypocrisy, while half-lies are acts of weakness. That means that half-truths are vile, while half-lies are pitiful. I figured that half-truths were far worse than lies and half-lies. And I concluded that half-truths, not lies, were the opposite of truth."

"You were a budding philosopher, Miss Sweet."

"Maybe. But there seemed more important things to do. Anyway, I got a C."

Jane closed the door to the compartment and leaned her elbows against the flimsy railing below the window. The train was wending its way through the mountains. A fast moving stream ran along the embankment. A red car bounced along the road that ran parallel to the stream. Skinny cows wandered among the weeds. Sheep clustered in the distance. Stocky sunburnt women—baba? mama?—kerchiefs tied tightly about their heads, bent over at the hips, plucked and dug in the gardens that sprang up, unexpectedly, along the tracks. For all she knew, her father may have been in the underground in this very place.

What was it like, tato? Tell me. I won't interrupt. The worst time is the spring, he says to us, a beer can in his hand, his legs stretched out, his feet in flip-flops. As the snow melts, the earth turns moist and the earthen walls leak, worms and rodents burrow through, everything smells of rotting leaves, mud clings to your clothes, your boots, your face and hands. The darkness seems darker, heavier, stickier. It is like being wrapped in your own filth. Not just for minutes or even hours, but for days, for weeks, for months. You cannot wipe it off, the filth, it clings to you, it sticks to you, it enters your pores and breathes into you. I crawl into the second chamber and sit in the corner near the air vent, breathing deeply. My head feels giddy from the pungent aroma of leaves and grass and melting snow. How is it outside? When was I last outside? Before the last snows fell, just before the forests and the meadows were covered with two meters of snow, we had climbed out at night, gingerly lifting the cover, listening for footsteps, shouts, and whispers—whispers were worst, they were most dangerous—turning our heads slowly from right to left and from left to right, listening intently, listening to the dark, listening to the trees, the leaves, the sky, and the stars, listening to everything but other human beings, because there was no one else to be seen, to be heard, and least of all to be spoken to. And hearing nothing, hearing only the wind, or the occasional hooting of an owl, we raise the cover, slowly, slowly, careful not to disturb the ground, careful not to break any branches. And then, we yank ourselves out of the hole, holding our breath, suppressing shouts of joy, suppressing our exhilaration, unable to contain our coughing and the tears flowing from eyes unused to moonlight. We sling our rifles over our left shoulders, our empty knapsacks over our right shoulders. Running from tree to tree, from bush to bush, avoiding muddy ground, avoiding twigs, avoiding the paths used by the peasants and the hollows favored by the boys and girls, avoiding the stream where women washed clothes, avoiding the wells where gossips gathered, heading furtively like thieves, like bandits, for the house farthest from the bunker, at the far end of the village. We stop at the edge of the forest, peering at the quiet house, its windows black, its walls a mournful, eerie gray. We stand silently, like ancient monuments to some unknown war dead, we stand so silently that you could almost see us move—*I can see you move, tato*—swaying like the tall grass at the edge of the lake where everyone used to fish and bathe. Ivanko crosses the clearing separating the forest from the house. *I know what happens next, tato.* Shouts break the tranquility. There are shots, from the left and from the right, and his shadow disappears. And then, just where it disappeared, it reappears, for half a second or even less, as a quick flash illuminates his open mouth, and the shadow disappears for good, to be replaced by other shadows and by more shouts. Quickly, silently, I step back into the forest. As I slide into my grave, replacing the cover, hoping, praying that the grass and the bushes fall exactly into place just as they were thirty minutes ago, I think of the filth and the darkness that awaits me at the bottom. The shouts come nearer, I can hear barking. *Watch it! I can see them. They are coming after you!* They are sweeping the forest, shooting randomly, poking their long rods into the earth, looking for pockets of emptiness under the ground. *Don't worry, tato, they won't find you. I won't let them.* And then nothing less than a miracle happens. The heavens open and pour water onto the forest, and into my hole, and when the water reaches my ankles and the filth becomes unbearable, I know that I am saved. By morning the water has turned to snow— a second miracle—and I know that the shouts and the dogs and the rods will not return until the snow melts and life returns to normal. *See, tato? Your story does have a happy end.*

The train picked up speed. They were beginning the descent into the flat plains of Transcarpathia. Jane slid the door open and reentered the compartment.

"I wanted to talk to you about what happens next, professor."

Bazarov looked up from his book.

"When we get to Chop, they'll lock us in the car. You know that, don't you?"

Bazarov nodded.

"And we'll stay here for about two hours—"

"Possibly even three."

"—or possibly even three, while they raise the train and replace the existing carriage with—"

"—with one that is appropriate for the width of European tracks. Please, Miss Sweet, I know all that. Perhaps you could finally tell me what, as you put it, happens next."

"We stay in the compartment until we cross to the Hungarian side. A car—from the embassy—will be waiting for us. It'll take us to Vienna."

"And I'll be safe?"

"I know *I'll* be safe," said Jane. "As to you, professor—I suppose it depends on whether you were doing your duty and telling the truth, doesn't it?"

As the train slowed down perceptibly, the conductor appeared in the doorway.

"We will be in Chop in five minutes," he said. "Prepare your passports. If you want to get out, you may do so. But you won't be able to reenter until the train is on the tracks again."

"Thank you," Jane said, "but we'll stay here."

"If you need to use the WC," he continued, "do so now. It'll be closed as well." The conductor went back to his end of the car.

"A few more hours," said Jane, looking at her watch, "and it's over."

"Are you nervous, Miss Sweet?"

"No, professor, I'm not. But you should be."

"And why is that, Miss Sweet? I feel quite safe in your embrace."

"Well, professor, if I were the assassin, this is where I'd kill you."

"Oh?" Bazarov raised his eyebrows. "Why do you say that?"

"We'll be sitting inside a train car for a long time." Jane relished the malice that was driving her. "Like sitting ducks." When will he start sweating?

"But no one can get in."

"And we can't get out. A trained marksman with a high-powered rifle—one shot, maybe two, and it's over."

"But the shades are lowered. You can't shoot what you can't see."

"A grenade launcher, then."

"But they'd kill you too. And the conductor."

"Your friend Kanapa wasn't alone, as I recall. As to me—the U.S. government calls that collateral damage."

"Aren't *you* afraid, Miss Sweet?"

"I'm terrified, professor. But they pay me for that. And you—are you afraid?"

Bazarov paused before replying. He appeared to be reflecting. The bastard, Jane thought. The bastard's going to bullshit me again.

"No, Miss Sweet, I am not."

"And why not, professor? Most people fear death."

"I will tell you, Miss Sweet," Bazarov said slowly. "I have lived a good life. If I had to die this very minute—yes, of course, I would regret it—but no, no, Miss Sweet, I would not fear it."

"You are a lucky man, professor. Your friends—do you think they were afraid of dying?"

"How would I know, Miss Sweet? Only they could have answered that question. But you, Miss Sweet, tell me why *you* are so afraid."

"According to your logic, it must be because I haven't lived a good life. And you know what, professor, for once I think you may be right."

"Ah," he said excitedly, "don't you see, Miss Sweet? You have just experienced an epiphany. This is the moment we intellectuals value above everything else—that moment of complete clarity, when everything suddenly seems perfectly obvious. This moment is very important, Miss Sweet, a turning point. Your life will never be the same. You are a very fortunate young woman, Miss Sweet."

"*If* I live."

"And if you do not, Miss Sweet? So what? You will at least have experienced this one moment of clarity."

"Well, yes, but I think I'd prefer remembering this moment, and not just experiencing it."

"No, Miss Sweet, memories are nothing. And experience is nothing. Only one thing is everything, Miss Sweet, and that is—"

"I know, I know—knowledge of the truth, right?"

"You are a fast learner, Miss Sweet. You should have been an intellectual."

The train pulled into Chop. Bazarov remained in the compartment, its shades lowered. Jane leaned back against the door. The platforms had been renovated, lamps had been installed, communist insignia had been removed, and three blue and yellow flags had been attached to the front of the station. Grease-stained workmen strolled about the tracks, several carried crowbars and other tools, one had a lantern of some kind, all wore dirty caps pulled down over their gritty faces. Some gesticulated, others lit cigarettes. They shouted to one another, but Jane couldn't make out what they were saying. Black-haired Gypsy women smoking cigarettes stood in the shadows. Their children ran about. In the distance Jane could see three border guards approaching the train. Sometime tonight she'd be back in Vienna. Bazarov would be handed over to the proper authorities and presumably taken back to the United States. She'd write a report, and that would be that. And then what? Back to business as usual in the embassy? Back to her daily jousts with Bristol? Back to the ambassador's insufferable monologues? Perhaps I *have* had an epiphany.

There was a loud knock on the door of the train car, and the conductor rose to his feet and ran to open it. Two border guards walked in and proceeded down the aisle in single file. Their footsteps resounded in the empty car. As they stopped just before Bazarov's compartment, Jane looked up at their faces.

"Anatoly!"

There was silence.

"I'm sorry," he said.

"For what?"

"For having to kill him."

Again there was silence.

"Be my guest," Jane said and walked quickly toward the other end of the car.

Jane smoked a cigarette and, after hearing three muffled shots, returned to her compartment. She knew what she had to do. It was time to join the big boys. The other guard had gone, but Filatov remained sitting inside. He was unscrewing the silencer as she walked in. *Sayonara, Mike. This one's for you, tato.*

"I should have known," she said. "I almost did, you know. You were too full of contradictions. You were impossible."

Flatov placed his gun in his holster.

"Your perfect Ukrainian, your Viennese mannerisms, your Soviet"—Jane stopped in mid-sentence—"Anatoly, you're from Lviv, aren't you?"

He said nothing.

"Of course you are."

"We came here after the war—"

"—to fight the nationalists."

Both fell silent.

"Tell me, Anatoly, did you always know about me?"

"Yes."

"How did you find out?"

"I have friends."

"The Ukrainians?"

"Yes."

"Official? Mafiya?"

"Yes."

"I see." She sat down next to Filatov. "So what happens now?"

"Now, I put away my gun and leave."

"Shouldn't you be killing me?"

"Yes, but I shall not."

"Why not? You're a professional, and I'm a loose end."

"You wouldn't understand."

"Try me."

"Because," Filatov seemed to be searching for words, "because communism is dead. That's why. Can you understand?"

"Yes, I think I can. Of course I wouldn't have let you kill me."

"I know," he said wearily. "It would have been a struggle, but in the end you would have been dead. Or me."

"How long have you been in the KGB, Anatoly? That *is* your name, isn't it?"

"Yes, I confess," he smiled. "Anatoly Sergeevich Filatov, at your service. *Küss die Hand, gnädige Frau.*" He bowed. "All my life."

"And your specialty was what? Wet work?"

He nodded.

"And how many imperialists have you eliminated?"

"Many, Miss Jane—"

"—call me Ivanka."

"Many, Ivanka, very, very many."

"You are a disillusioned agent. You should have lived in the thirties."

"Probably."

"But then you would have been a mass murderer."

"Probably."

"But at least you would have been a happy, a contented mass murderer."

"We all try to believe in something, Ivanka. Without belief, what are we?"

"What we are with belief—human beings."

"No." He shook his head. "Belief makes us human. Without belief we are animals. With belief we can choose between right and wrong. We can even define right and wrong. Without belief we can only rely on our instincts."

"Funny," Jane said. "The man you just killed said something very similar. You were birds of a feather, Anatoly."

"Not quite, Ivanka. That man stole money and sold women. For what? For himself. I did what I did—"

"You killed."

"Yes, I killed, but not for myself, not because it was good or convenient or useful for me. I killed for a higher cause."

"Communism."

"Yes, communism. And what is wrong with that, Ivanka?"

"It doesn't work. It killed millions of people."

"And your capitalism? It works and it kills millions of people. Who is the opportunist and who is the idealist, Ivanka? The one who supports a lost cause or the one who jumps on the bandwagon?"

"Capitalism never constructed the Gulag, Anatoly. Even you should know that."

"Capitalism *is* a Gulag, Ivanka. You should know that."

Jane lit a cigarette and offered one to Filatov.

"And what will you do now, Anatoly?"

"Well, first I shall have to explain to my Ukrainian friends why I did not shoot you. They will be happy, actually. The deeply democratic Ukrainian state does not need a diplomatic scandal with the United States. Then I shall go home. To Moscow. My vacation will soon be over and I shall have to return to the Federal Security Service. I am," he said dryly, "a highly respected and variously distinguished colonel. I am a hero. I have a uniform with rows of medals. I have a big desk and," he smiled, "I have many phones."

"Are there children waiting for you?"

"No. Alas, no. I am one of those agents who took that slogan literally—the Party is my family, the Party is my life."

"The iron Bolshevik. Right, Anatoly?"

"The iron Bolshevik. The man of steel."

"But now cracked and corroded."

"And covered with rust," he added. "And disintegrating rapidly."

"Did you ever think of defecting? Especially now. I mean, it's all over."

"Ah, Ivanka, but that's the problem. Then, when there was communism, I would never have betrayed the cause. But now, when there is no more communism, there is nothing to betray and no reason to defect."

"For the lifestyle. Why not for a better life, Anatoly?"

"What would an iron Bolshevik do with a better life? No, then it was too early, now it is too late. Like for you."

"Like for me?"

"Yes. *We* are birds of a feather, Ivanka. We are both victims of communism's death. But the war is over. History has ended. There is nothing left to do."

"Is there no communism-*ness*, Anatoly?"

Filatov laughed.

"Alas, no. Dima, at least in this instance, was wrong."

"Then there is no salvation for you, Anatoly. You *do* know that, don't you?"

Filatov nodded.

"You know what I am, Ivanka? A whiskey priest."

Jane had to smile at the analogy.

"Then there's only one way out for you, Anatoly. You must know that, too."

Filatov shook his head.

"No, Ivanka, I fear I shall die, old and defeated, in my bed."

"It's too bad that you can't live without belief, Anatoly. When I was a kid, we used to grow all kinds of vegetables in our backyard. Tomatoes, cucumbers, lettuce, peas—everything. I hated it, but it gave my parents strength."

"I am not made for tending gardens, Ivanka. You should know that. I accept that such an activity can give meaning. But it is not for me. I don't just know that here"—he pointed to his head—"I also know that here, in my heart."

"You are a dinosaur, Anatoly."

"I know." He laughed. "Like Soviet heavy industry, I am slated for extinction. And you, Ivanka—what will you do?"

"I am not slated for extinction. It's back to Vienna for me. I think."

"Is there anything for you to do there? As a diplomat, I mean."

"No, not really. It's not like the days of the cold war. Vienna is quiet. A ghost town. But the opera is good, the cafes are nice. Perhaps I'll write my autobiography."

"So this case"—he paused—"this case has been a welcome distraction. Perhaps you should even thank me for the adventure."

"Perhaps."

"Of course, you too are a dinosaur. The cold war is over, Ivanka. There is no salvation for you either."

"No, Anatoly, you're wrong, dead wrong. For me there is. For me there definitely is."

Jane looked at her watch.

"We shall be moving in under an hour," she said. "Will you stay until then?"

"Yes."

"Then fuck me one last time."

They took off their clothes slowly, almost methodically. He piled his in one corner, she hers in another. Then she straddled him and they kissed, her arms holding his head, his arms about her torso. Soon, it was over. He lay with his head between her thighs, his lips pressed to her moist hair. Finally, he rose to his feet and she sat upright. They dressed in silence. As Filatov finished tying his shoelaces, Jane opened her purse.

"I'm sorry, Anatoly."

"For what?"

She pressed the gun to his temple and gently squeezed the trigger.

"For this."

0-595-34367-8

Find
oculist
address
on map
         quest

Printed in the United States
52668LVS00005B/313-327

9 780595 343676